THE HOTHOUSE
BY THE EAST RIVER

By the Same Author

MURIEL SPARK

The Hothouse
by the East River

THE VIKING PRESS / NEW YORK

THE HOTHOUSE
BY THE EAST RIVER

Chapter One

If it were only true that all's well that ends well, if only it were true.

She stamps her right foot.

She says, "I'll try the other one," sitting down to let the salesman lift her left foot and nicely interlock it with the other shoe.

He says, "They fit like a glove." The voice is foreignly correct and dutiful.

She stands, now, and walks a little space to the mirror, watching first the shoes as she walks, and then, half-turning, her leg's reflection. It is a hot, hot day of July in hot New York. She looks next at the heel.

She looks over at the other shoes on the floor beside the chair, three of them beside their three open boxes and two worn shoes lying on their sides. Finally, she glances at the salesman.

He focuses his eyes on the shoes.

Now, once more, it is evening and her husband has come in.

She sits by the window, speaking to him against the purr of the air conditioner, but looking away—out across the East River as if he were standing in the air beyond the windowpane. He stands in the middle of the room behind her and listens.

She says, "I went shopping. I went to a shoe store for some shoes. You won't believe me, what happened."

He says, "Well, what was it?"

She says, "You won't believe me, that's the trouble. You aren't sure that you'll believe me."

"How do I know if you don't tell me what it is?"

"You'll believe me, yes, but you won't believe that it really happened. What's the use of telling you? You don't feel sure of my facts."

"Oh tell me anyway," he says, as if he is not really interested.

"Paul," she says, "I recognised a salesman in a shoe store today. He used to be a prisoner of war in England."

"Which P.O.W.?"

"Kiel."

"Which Kiel?"

"Helmut Kiel. Which one do you think?"

"There was Claus, also Kiel."

"Oh, that little mess, that lop-sided one who read the books on ballet?"

"Yes, Claus Kiel."

"Well I'm not talking about him. I'm talking about Helmut Kiel. You know who I mean by 'Kiel.' Why have you brought up Claus Kiel?"

Paul thinks: She doesn't turn her head, she watches the East River.

One day he thought he had caught her, in profile, as he

moved closer to her, smiling at Welfare Island as if it were someone she recognised. The little island was only a mass of leafage, seen from the window. She could not possibly have seen a person so far away down there.

Is it possible that she is smiling again, he thinks; could she be smiling to herself, retaining humorous reflections to herself? Is she sly and sophisticated, not mad after all? But it isn't possible, he thinks; she is like a child, the way she comes out with everything at this hour of the evening.

She tells him everything that comes into her head at this hour of the evening and it is for him to discover whether what she says is true or whether she has imagined it. But has she decided on this course, or can't she help it? How false, how true?

It is true that in the past winter he has seemed to catch her concealing a smile at the red Pepsi-Cola sign on the far bank of the river. Now he thinks of the phrase, "tongue in cheek," and is confused between what it means and how it would work if Elsa, with her head averted towards the river, actually put her tongue in her cheek, which she does not.

And Paul, still standing in the middle of the carpet, then looks at her shadow. He sees her shadow cast on the curtain, not on the floor where it should be according to the position of the setting sun from the window bay behind her, cross-town is the West Side. He sees her shadow, as he has seen it many times before, cast once more unnaturally. Although he has expected it, he turns away his head at the sight.

"Paul," she says, still gazing at the river, "go and get us a drink."

Their son, Pierre, came to see them last night. He said, while they were discussing, by habit, in the hall, the problem of Mother: "She is not such a fool."

"Then I am the fool, to spend my money on Garven."

"She's got to have Garven." He uttered this like a threat, intensifying his voice to scare away the opposition that he knew to be prowling.

Garven Bey is her analyst. Pierre is anxious that his mother should not go back into the clinic and so upset his peace of mind. Moreover, Pierre knows it was not his father's money that went so vastly on Garven, but the surface-dust, the top silt, merely, of his mother's fortune.

Last night, Paul said, as his son was leaving, "What did you think she looked like tonight?"

"All right. There's definitely something strange, of course. . . ."

Paul said good night abruptly, almost satisfied that his son had still not noticed the precise cause of the strangeness.

Paul cannot acknowledge it. A mirage, that shadow of hers. Not a fact.

She gazes out of the window. "Paul, go and get a drink."

But Paul stands on. He says to her as she sits by the window, "Are you serious about this man in the shoe shop?"

"Yes."

"Then, Elsa, I should say you have imagined Helmut Kiel. This is in the imaginative category, almost definitely. You couldn't have come across him in a shoe store. He died in prison with only himself to thank for it. You should tell Garven of this experience."

"All right."

"What shoe shop was it?"

"Melinda's at Madison Avenue. At least I think so."

"Are you smiling, there?"

"No. Why don't you make a drink?"

"He died in prison six, seven years after the war."

She laughs. Then she says, "I see what you mean."

"What?"

"Plainly you are not speaking literally."

"I think I'll have a drink." But he does not go. He thinks, She has become a mocker, she wasn't always like this. It's I who have made her so.

She sits immobile; and now, to his mind, she is real estate like the source of her money. She sits, well-dressed with her pretty hair-do and careful make-up, but sits solidly, as on valuable land-property painted up like a deteriorating building that has not yet been pulled down to make way for those high steel structures, her daughter and her son. So Paul's mind ripples over the surface.

And he thinks to himself, deliberately, word by word: I must pull myself together. She is mad.

The Pan Am sign on the far bank of the river flicks on and off. She seems to be catching a sudden unexpected glimpse of the United Nations building, which has been standing there all the time, and she shudders.

"Are you cold?" he says. "These air conditioners are too old. They aren't right."

"They can be treacherous," she says.

"Elsa," he says, "do you feel chilly? Why don't we get a modern system?"

She laughs out of the window.

He speaks again, meaning to win her round, meaning to insinuate an idea into her head that might fetch her back to reason, presuming she is departing from reason once more.

"The temperature touched a hundred and one degrees

at noon. The highways have buckled, many places."

She has turned her head towards the dark mass of Welfare Island.

He feels he has probably failed in his attempt to say, "You are suffering from the heat, your imagination . . ." He feels he might be wrong, he is not sure, as yet, if she is going to have a relapse. This has happened before, he thinks, here in this room I have stood, she has sat, how many times?

He says, "What's the name of the shoe store?"

"Melinda's, Madison Avenue somewhere near Fifty-fifth, Fifty-sixth—might be Fifty-seventh."

He says, "Upper Fifties and Madison. It still can't be less than ninety-eight."

She says to the East River: "He means ninety-eight degrees—the temperature." Then, still looking out of the window, she says, "Paul, get me a drink. I'll have vodka on the rocks, please."

She is looking for something out there. The sun has gone down. Yes, she is looking out for it again. Silently Paul says to himself, "It's not there." And again, "There's nothing there."

"The heat out there has affected you," she says, her face still turned to the dark blue river where it quivers with the ink-red reflection of the Pepsi-Cola sign on the opposite bank. "It's affected you, Paul," she says in her tranquillity. "You've been standing there in that spot since you came in." She has moved her head very little to the right and now she is looking at the United Nations building with its patches of lighted windows. "Since you came in," she says, "you've been standing there watching me, Paul. It's the heat making you suspicious. Today's been the hottest on record for twelve years. Tomorrow is to be worse. People are going mad in the streets. People coming home, men coming home, will have riots in their hearts and heads, never mind riots in the streets."

He wants to go and prepare their drinks, and has been thinking, This has happened before, but he will not move lest she should think she has taunted him into it. He says, "Why did you go shopping for shoes in the heat?"

"I had swollen feet. I needed a bigger size."

The cunning answers of the crazy. . . . He turns, now, and goes into the kitchen for the ice. Will she incline her face towards him when he comes back?

He breaks up the ice in the kitchen, he lingers. Eventually he returns, with face and eyes strained in the effort.

New York, home of the vivisectors of the mind, and of the mentally vivisected still to be reassembled, of those who live intact, habitually wondering about their states of sanity, and home of those whose minds have been dead, bearing the scars of resurrection: New York heaves outside the consultant's office, agitating all around her about her ears.

He looks across from his armchair to hers (for he does not believe in the couch; to relinquish it had been his first speciality) and says, "And then?"

"I came to Carthage."

"Carthage?"

She says, "I could write a book."

"What do you mean by Carthage?" he says. "You say you came. You came, you say. Do you mean here is Carthage?"

"Here?"

He says, "Well sort of."

"No, it was only a manner of speaking." She smiles to herself, as if to irritate him. He is thrown, knowing vaguely that Carthage was an ancient city of ancient times but unable to gather together all at once the many things he has probably heard about Carthage.

She says, in the absence of his reply, "I think I'm really all right, Garven." Garven is his first name. His claim is "I can get my patients right away on to a first-name basis"; it is the second on the list of his specialities.

"I'm all right, Garven," she says again while he is still wending his way towards Carthage.

"Yes, I hope so. But we've got a good bit of ground to cover yet, Elsa, you know."

She says, as if to irritate him, "Why do you say 'cover'? Isn't that a peculiar word for you to use? I thought psychiatry was meant to uncover something. But you say 'cover.' You said, 'We've got a good bit of ground to cover yet—' "

"I know, I know." He places his hands out before him, palms downward, to hush her up. He then explains the meaning of "cover up" in its current social usage; he explains bitterly with extreme care.

She says, "You aren't getting annoyed, are you?"

"Me? No."

She says, "I came to Carthage where there bubbled around me in my ears a cauldron of unholy loves."

"Elsa," he says, "just take it easy. Relax, you have to relax."

Arriving home she says, "I managed to rattle Garven again today." She curves herself into the most comfortable chair, with her back to the window, and smiling into the reflection of sky in the glass of a picture, as if congratulating it. "I rattled him. He said he wanted to establish a person-to-person relationship with me."

Paul says, "Have you nothing better to do with your money than waste your doctor's time with it?"

"Not much." Then she adds, "Tra-la-la," to the simple notes of doh-ray-mee.

"I wouldn't be in his shoes. I wouldn't like to have to read a woman," Paul says.

She laughs half-privately; at least she does not go near the window and share the joke with whatever it is out there on the East River, invisible to everyone but herself, that she takes such notice of through the windowpane, day after day.

He says, "I went along to the shoe store."

"Did you see him?"

"Yes, it was Kiel, all right."

"Helmut Kiel," she says.

"Yes, Helmut Kiel."

She says, "Not Claus, you see."

"No, Helmut Kiel."

"So you see, it wasn't my imagination," she says.

"Elsa, I never said it was your imagination, Elsa. Sometimes you imagine things. I just had to be sure, that's all, Elsa. It was certainly put out that he died in prison. There's some mystery about him. Always was."

She laughs and is over by the window again, as he had feared, in the attitude of communing with a sort of friend about the high humour of what he has just said. He stands in the middle of the room.

"Did Kiel recognise you, Elsa?"

"I think so. Did he recognise you?"

"No, I saw him through the window from the street. He didn't see me."

"Are you sure?" she says.

It is better when she says something than nothing when she sits by the window, although when she speaks it's likely to be bad. Because she usually says something ordinary, as if everything were all right.

Everything is not all right.

"Sit by one of the other windows, Elsa, for a change."

"There's nothing to see from the other windows."

"Well, there's the street, isn't there? And the people, the traffic."

He knows, now, that she has been smiling.

"Oh for God's sake, Elsa, why sit by the bloody window at all?"

He pronounces bloody as "blawdy," this being a word he has not learned as a child in Montenegro from his English governess. "Bloody" he had learned from the English during the war when his ear was no longer receptive. Apart from such late encounters with the vernacular his English is good. He is sure she is smiling out to the river. "The bloody window all day."

And he says, "You're still a young woman, Elsa. Sitting by windows all day . . ." He has said this before. Sometimes it seems certain that she knows he is not being honest. But there is something else he is concealing as he speaks. Perhaps she knows it.

"Not all day," she says. "I sit here mostly late afternoon, mostly in the evening." This happens to be true.

The window bay of the room, jutting out fourteen stories above everything, is considered to be a feature of luxury. These great windows cover a third of the east wall which overlooks the river, the whole of the north wall towards the street, and the adjoining corner of the west wall from where can be seen the length of the street with the intersection of avenues diminishing in the distance as far as the Pan Am building. Within the rectangular space are the plants and ferns which any normal person would put there.

Sometimes there is a marvellous sunset pouring in the west window, but Elsa prefers to watch the river. The sunset from the west spills the shadows of Elsa's palms and ferns all over the floor, all over Elsa and the curtains by the east window. Out of the west window, on good days at sunset the Manhattan rooflines are black against the brilliance while the sky over the East River darkens slowly.

He cannot remember exactly what it was that, on returning to the flat at seven in the evening—or six . . . if he could remember the season of the year . . .

In the evening—he can not exactly remember the day, the time of day, perhaps it was spring, or winter, perhaps it was five, six o'clock . . .

He is standing in the middle of the room. She is sitting by the window, staring out over the East River. The late sunlight from the opposite window touches her shoulders and hair, it casts the shadow of palm leaves across the carpet, over her arm. The chair she sits in casts a shadow before her.

There is another shadow, hers. It falls behind her.

Behind her, and cast by what light? She is casting a shadow in the wrong direction. There's no light shining upon her from the east window, it comes from the west window. What is she looking at?

He looks. Welfare Island. The borough of Queens across the river. The river moving past a moored barge.

She says, without turning her head, "Why are you standing there? Why don't you get a drink?"

Or she says, "Pierre just left."

Or, "I bought a pair of shoes today."

The day is getting darker. He switches on the floor lamp, although the room is still light enough.

Her shadow does not move. He comes and stands beside her, looking out. There is no beam of light coming in from the East River or the sky. But she goes on looking and receiving; perhaps she's begun to smile. She casts a shadow behind her as she moves her chair to make room for him. Today she began a new course of analysis, or perhaps she began last week.

She is saying, "I bought a pair of shoes."

Or, "Pierre doesn't know what to do."

Or, "Katerina ran out of deodorant in Castellammare."

Paul turns to go to the kitchen for ice. At the door he turns again.

His heart thumps for help. "Help me! Help me!" cries his heart, battering the sides of the coffin. "The schizophrenic has imposed her will. Her delusion, her figment, her nothing-there, has come to pass."

"Did Kiel recognise you, Elsa?"

"I think so. I saw Garven today."

"I'm in danger from Kiel, and all you can talk about is your own problem."

"I don't have a problem. It was your idea that I should go to Garven."

He is dressing; she comes through from her bathroom into her bedroom.

"Garven has the problem anyway," she says. "The problem of me is his, not mine—" The light from his table falls upon her. Her shadow bends towards it.

He holds his breath— "Let me out! Let me out!"

He will not sleep beside her in bed any more. Never again, never again. No man can sleep with a woman whose shadow falls wrong and who gets light or something from elsewhere.

He watches her walk into her bedroom. The last time they dined out the hostess had to fuss with the candles at the table, which was unaccountably darkened over. Or was it the time before that? The last time, maybe, was when they were all looking at the newly acquired Kandinsky: "Just stand aside a little, Elsa—Paul—standing in the light? There's a shadow . . . who? . . . how?"

Nobody has really noticed it, and yet everyone has noticed it. Pierre and Katerina—perhaps they have talked of it between themselves:

"Mother is terrifying. Have you seen how her shadow falls?" No, they wouldn't say that. Pierre would telephone to Garven, perhaps. No, Garven would think him crazy.

Has Garven noticed?

No, Garven is too busy with his problem.

Paul shouts into the bedroom, "You don't care what happens to me! Can't you realise what it means, that Kiel is alive and has come here to New York?"

"Have him checked," she replies in a practical voice as if it were a question of a cavity in a tooth.

"I've had him checked," he shouts. "He's got every cover. There's a Helmut Kiel, deceased, on the prison records at Hamburg. He's got a new name, obviously; new papers, a job in a shoe store, everything. What do you care?"

He feels easier after this row. Helmut Kiel is a definite danger to his life, but preferable to the torture of that something of Elsa's out there on the river.

"Are you ready?" he says.

Or perhaps he says, "Now, pull yourself together."

She says, "I'm ready, are you? I don't have a problem. Katerina . . ."

Pierre's apartment in East Seventy-sixth Street is beautifully cool this summer. Paul envies the silent air-conditioning system of his son's apartment, distributed from a noiseless central equipment throughout the house, and once more decides to move from the apartment by the East River down there in Forty-fourth Street where the air conditioners hum separately in each room.

"Look," says Paul, "it was before you were born, a long time ago."

"But, Father, be reasonable and methodical, that's all I say. See a lawyer. Have the F.B.I. make a thorough investigation. And if you can't leave it at that, have a private firm investigate the man."

Paul does not want to leave this evenly cool apartment. He lingers, even having said all he has wanted to say, even to the point of beginning again. "It was when your mother and I were young, in England, during the war. . . ."

The apartment is cool in its decorations. Very little furniture, like a psychiatrist's consulting room. Elsa has said she enjoys a sense of repose when she visits her analyst.

"Then I've got the problem of your mother on top of it," Paul says.

"Leave that to Garven. It's Garven's problem."

"Oh is it? Oh, is it Garven's problem?" Paul says. "Sometimes I wonder."

"Wonder what?" says Pierre with a sudden stare that betokens, surely, an innocent question.

"Have you ever thought there was something strange about your mother?" Paul says.

"Yes. What else does she see Garven for? But we shouldn't let her go away again. Not into the clinic, not there. It isn't necessary. Not with modern drugs and therapy and so on." Pierre is anxious for him to leave; he has something else to do, or is perhaps afraid that his father will say too much.

"I think about Kiel, real name Mueller, that's the main problem," Paul says. "Anything you can think of, let me know. I just wanted to put you in the picture, Pierre, in case anything happens to me."

"Don't worry." Pierre looks out of the window.

Pierre, looking out of the window, resembles his mother more than usual.

His shadow falls in folds on the curtain, cast by the lamp behind him, his shadow falls where it should fall. It moves as Pierre moves. The father says, "I want you to have the whole picture, Pierre." He watches his son's movements as if almost hoping the tall young man could cause things to happen by the mere waving of that wand, his body.

"I have the picture, I think."

"Yes, but the picture, the whole picture and nothing but the picture," Paul says. "Pierre, it's a complex matter. If your mother can't rouse herself or feel anything about my predicament with Kiel, then I'm in all the greater danger, Pierre."

Pierre looks round, briefly and with an irritated opening of his lips, as if to say, "Don't 'Pierre' me." After a while he sits down and says, "Mother is no fool. She doesn't panic, that's all."

"Panic! I don't say she ought to panic. I say she might show some concern. After all, she saw the man. It was your mother who first saw him in the shoe store. She simply told me. She sat there calmly and told me, as if it were something as meaningless as a pair of shoes."

"Shoes have meaning, Father."

Paul wants to hit his son, and scream at him that his rotten education has made him unfit for the modern world, and it has been his mother's rotten money that has sent him the rounds of the world to every school of art history that money can buy. Paul lays his palms on the arms of his chair and, for the usual reason that deters people from violence of word and deed, refrains from it. He says, "She sits looking out. She remembers Kiel very well. She remembers what happened when we were engaged during the war. She knows that Kiel was a double agent and went to prison after the war. She heard that he died in prison and now she's seen him in New York. But if one makes any appeal to her sense of its significance she's not interested. She's away and out of reach. She looks out of the window and I stand there like a grocer who's come to demand payment of an overdue bill from, say, Michelangelo while he's up on the scaffold of the Sistine Chapel, painting the ceiling. She says, 'Go and get a drink.' That's what she says, and I'm only a little figure far beneath her and her thoughts."

Pierre looks interested at last, either because he is interested or because he is intelligent enough to put up a show at this point. He has turned from the window and has sat in the chair opposite Paul, his left arm so placed on the arm-rest, perhaps by intention, that he can see the time at a glance.

Pierre says, "She's more—" before the doorbell rings. He

raises his eyebrows, rises, and goes to press the button that will release the street door. He returns for the few moments that it takes for the lift to ascend, now speculating on who the visitor can be. He lets in a flabby pale-fleshed man with a crew cut and sandy pink-rimmed eyes, wearing pale-blue trousers and a loose white shirt hanging over them. Paul can not decide upon his age, the man's features being packed away in flesh.

His name is Peregrine. Perhaps it is his first or middle name, perhaps his last. "Peregrine—my father. Father—Peregrine," Pierre says.

"I have to go," says Paul.

As Pierre lets his father out he says, "I doubt very much that the man you've seen here in New York is the Kiel you've been talking about. I think you've made some mistake."

Chapter Two

Three years ago, Elsa said, "Perhaps I'm imagining things, as Caesar said to his wife at dawn on the Ides of March."

"Oh, come now," Paul said. "There's a difference between your case and his."

On that occasion Pierre and Katerina had been in the room. Katerina was starting her last college vacation.

"Where did you read that about Caesar?" Katerina said.

"Oh, how you bore me," said her mother. "So bloody literal."

Katerina said, "I don't understand, Mother."

"We're not all gifted with understanding," Elsa said, and fixed her gaze on the windows.

"You used to be different towards us," Pierre said. "You used to be sweet and patient. Not that it matters."

"There's a time for everything. It's your turn to be sweet and patient," Elsa said.

"They show a lot of sweetness and a lot of patience, Elsa," said Paul. "And," he said, "I try my best, too."

"Where did you read that about Caesar, Mother?" Katerina said.

"I didn't read it."

"Then how do you know he said it?"

Elsa laid her forehead on the window. She started to laugh. The father left the room; the daughter followed, then the son.

That was only three years ago. But now it is long years ago, when they are recently engaged and are working together in England at the Compound, during the second world war. The Compound is a small outpost of British Intelligence in the heart of the countryside. Paul says to Elsa, "Did you hear what happened to Kiel?"

"No—what?" she says.

"He's been sent back to the prisoner-of-war camp."

"Which Kiel? You mean Claus Kiel?" she says.

"Oh, him—no, no not him, he's harmless. I mean Helmut."

"But I saw Helmut last night. He was here."

"Yes, well he was sent back this morning."

"What for?" she says.

"He started a fight in his billet, apparently. Smashed a window."

"Helmut smashed a window? Last night?—But that's not like him, you know. He's a serious type, Paul. Someone must have provoked him."

"No," Paul says, "they didn't."

"Well, why did he start the fight?" she says.

"He must have wanted to be sent back to camp. The bloody fools here don't see that. All they care about are the regulations. They've got no psychology. The German workers have got to keep order, so he's been sent back to the camp for bad conduct—which is obviously what he wanted."

"Why should he want to go back?" she says.

"I don't know. I thought you might know."

She starts walking over to the hut where they work and he walks with her. The spring sun has come out. She pulls the wide belt of her dress tighter into her waistline and slings the short strap of her bag over her shoulder. She says, "There could be a lot of reasons. It isn't our business, it's for Security to find out."

He says, "They don't seem to think he had any reason to want to get out of working for us. They seem to think he just lost control and broke out into violence."

She stops at the door of the hut. She looks in the doorway and speaks with her head still turned away from him.

"Well maybe he did just lose control. Prisoners often do," she says, "for one does forget sometimes that these German collaborators are still prisoners."

"But I wouldn't have thought Kiel would lose control as easily as that, would you?"

"No, I wouldn't quite honestly. It's a shock."

"When did you see him last night?" Paul says.

"He was here, working— Where do you think I saw him? Where else would you think?"

"I said 'when' not 'where.' I'm not suggesting that you've broken any rules, Elsa. I'm not a Security officer."

She says, "He was here till midnight and went home on the bus with the others. He was perfectly all right, then. Perfectly cheerful. Perfectly. . . . Of course it must be nerve-racking for them when they know all the time they've ratted on their own country. I don't know what to think, really. What do you think?"

Paul looks at the clock on the wall inside the doorway,

and says he has to go. He looks at her as if to ask if she has anything more to say.

She says, "Let me know if you hear anything more, won't you, Paul?"

"Are you having supper in the canteen?"

"Yes, but I won't get away till nine."

"I'll see you there at nine," he says.

The Compound is hard asphalt in the primrose light, early spring of 1944, England.

"I'm a spent volcano. Just a slag-heap with a hole down the middle and a thin wisp of curly smoke coming up out of my hair."

So she drawls, in these days of her languid vigour, while Paul takes off his sun-glasses, breathes on the lenses, and wipes them with his pocket handkerchief, one by one; then he puts on the glasses again, but still cannot understand the girl.

Not long afterwards, Paul is called in for questioning by a Security officer.

This Security officer, Colonel Tylden, has been appointed sagely. He is a military man with a limited imagination which, even in its limited capacity, he seldom uses. Consequently he is less likeable, less highly regarded but more just and more efficient than other, more brilliant and subtle, investigators whose courteous looks and hysterical hearts combine to put up a brilliant performance in the course of interrogation, but who probe so often in directions deviating from facts to which they never return.

"Sit down."

Paul sits down.

"Elsa," says the man, "slept with Kiel."

Paul frowns, and, looking out of the upper pane of the window, gives a sigh of exasperation which is meant to convey the fact that he knows the colonel's methods and is not to be impressed.

The colonel says, "Which of course you know."

"No," says Paul wearily, "and neither do you."

The man shrugs his eyebrows. He starts afresh: "Not Claus Kiel, of course. Helmut."

Paul smiles at this truism within the hypothesis that Elsa has slept with anyone called Kiel. Paul's smile is tense, soon ended. But the officer then grants a long-drawn smile and says, "Yes, of course. An unnecessary distinction in this context. We can hardly suspect little Claus of having a girl in his bunker."

"Bunker? How could they have sex in the bunker, with anyone liable to come in? And those cots—narrow . . ."

He is thinking of the narrow sleeping-berths set up in the small rooms where the late-duty workers may rest between broadcasts.

"She used to go and rest in the bunker, Kiel's bunker. She admits that. Apparently she went in frequently between transmissions."

"Oh well, I haven't been on late duty for months, so I really couldn't say about that. I wouldn't have attached importance to it, anyway. Elsa obviously doesn't."

"Why not?"

"She hasn't mentioned to me anything about resting in a bunker, or anything about Kiel or Kiel's bunker." Paul knows, as soon as he has spoken, the feebleness of this protest. He looks at the Security man, waiting for his gentle smile of sympathy for one deceived in love.

But the man behaves well and responds in a serious tone,

although, of course he can only say, "It's understandable that she hasn't mentioned it."

"And equally," says Paul, "understandable that she hasn't mentioned it if it means nothing to her, going into Kiel's bunker for a lie-down." He is immediately aware of his error in uttering that "if." He adds, "Since it means nothing to her." And he is about to elaborate further on Elsa's innocence when he realises that the interrogator is now waiting for a real outburst of that indignation which expresses inner doubts. Paul remembers he is a foreigner and decides to shut up.

The man waits long enough, hopefully, before speaking again. He states, "You and Elsa—there has been a little estrangement lately."

"No," says Paul, as if answering a question.

"You haven't been about together so much, lately."

Paul looks at him in a puzzled manner.

The man looks away, and, as if making a rather sad observation, says, "You don't see much of each other these days."

"Very true," says Paul, and is not to be drawn into what the man already knows. Formerly, Paul was able to go for long daily walks with Elsa in the countryside surrounding the Compound. Elsa was then on night duty and he on afternoon duty, so that their free time at the Compound coincided by two busy hours only; but their leave has always been arranged to coincide, so that they can go up to London for four days each fortnight, as they do, staying at the Strand Palace Hotel.

"I mean," says the man in answer to the silence, "that you aren't seen together as much as you used to be. Of course, you take your leave together, but I mean to say,

Elsa, of course, went on late duty at her own request."

"Not true," Paul says, taking no chances.

The officer opens a desk and takes out a bunch of keys, then he rises and goes over to the filing cabinet, where he inserts and turns a key. Paul is not sure if the cabinet drawer has not opened a little too easily, he is not sure if it was locked in the first place. The man has removed a blue cardboard file and is flipping through the papers inside it. He stops at one paper, half-removes it for a moment and concentrates his eyes upon it. Then he replaces the paper neatly, replaces the folder, shuts the drawer, locks it, tries it, and returns to his desk. There, he opens the drawer and replaces the keys.

He says, "She applied for late duty," and takes out a pocket notebook in which he writes something in pencil.

Paul says nothing. The performance looks unlikely, but it might equally well be genuine. Elsa had complained to him about being put on night duty, she had said she was trying to get out of it, and later had told him she had failed; it was her turn to work for six months on a shift beginning at four in the afternoon and ending some time between midnight and two o'clock the next morning.

The officer puts the notebook back in his pocket. He taps the desk with the pencil; he holds it between his first and middle fingers, and lets it tap lightly, first with the point and then, turning it, with the blunt end, as if tapping a cigarette at both ends. Tap, goes the little pencil. He says, "Thank you, Paul." He casts the pencil aside, and rises.

"Not at all, Colonel." Paul gets up to go and, between the chair and the door, is about to utter a curt request to be addressed more formally, when he decides sharply that he might sound like a chauffeur, tangled with umbrage, carping that his name is Mister. He withdraws silently, tangled indeed, but without having assumed inferiority.

Nor does he call off work for the rest of the day and go back to flop in his billet as he longs to do. He takes a bus as far as it can take him towards the Compound. Then he walks the rest of the distance, straight through two villages over a distance of four and a half miles. The gate-keeper greets him, "Fine day, sir," then looks at his watch as Paul walks past. "It's going to rain, though," says Paul, looking up at a collection of white clouds. There is no reason why the man should not look at his watch, but Paul forbears to look back and see whether the man is returning to the gate-house, there perhaps to telephone, under orders, to report Paul's arrival, and the time of it. It is just possible, it is infinitely possible, even probable, that Colonel Tylden, the Security officer, has wanted to find out how far Paul has been put off his stroke. However, Paul's jitters are not available to human eyes this afternoon in the early spring of England, 1944.

"So I said to John, if Harry and Giselle come with us, Howard can go with Harry to Pearl's and John could come with Gene for the Sunday night before we leave. But if Ray stops over at Nantucket then I have to be there for Merlin and Jay as they have nowhere to go. That's if Pierre goes to Italy. If not I don't know what we can do. I know Katerina can't be back till September, but suppose Pierre comes the last week in August, then we've got to find somewhere for Jay or Merlin, one or the other. But John said let them go to California and get a vacation job like Elaine Harvey and Sam last summer. Why land on us? Garven says—"

"Who are you talking to?" says Paul.

"You," says Elsa, her eyes still fixed on the East River. "We've got to plan, we've left it late enough and the house will be overcrowded if all these people come to light. Garven says I'll make myself ill."

"What's going on out there?" Paul says, coming boldly to look out of the window over her shoulders.

"Don't shout," she says.

"I wasn't shouting," he replies, softening his voice which hardened a moment ago with the effort of approaching her look-out station in the window alcove. He says, "A lot of mist this evening."

"Really?" she says, as if she cannot see for herself the heat-fog that has lowered over the city of New York all day.

He withdraws, sideways and backwards, and stands at a distance from the window between one sofa and another.

He says, "Where did John call from?"

"Some campus, I think. It was just before lunch."

"Who is John, anyway? John who? And all those kids, who are they?"

"I didn't ask," she says. "They might be anybody."

"I'm sorry I took that house," Paul says.

She says, "If you want me to go into a clinic just as an excuse to put them off, nothing doing."

"Who's talking about a clinic? For God's sake, Elsa. It's one of your bad days, isn't it?"

She puts her head on one side and makes her eyes wide, flirtatiously, at the window. She says, "Yes, but I feel better already since you came in. Just in that short space I feel better already. What about a drink?"

Paul says to his son, "Pierre, your mother's anxious about the prospect of having too many people to stay this summer."

"Keep them away," says Pierre. "These people don't exist as far as I'm concerned."

"But it's her anxiety—she has these fits of worrying. Then it's all over as soon as she has a chance to talk to me. She needs my presence."

"Oh, they all worry about people coming to stay. All women do—everyone does. I do."

"Why isn't she anxious about me? I'm in danger," says Paul.

"Look," says Pierre wildly. "Talk to Garven. I'm not an expert on these feelings."

"My God, it's a rational normal fear. Why should I talk to Garven?" Paul says. And he thinks, as one who hopes to still the tempest: Now let us turn to something else. "Listen to me," his voice is saying. . . . In the summer of 1944, he is telling his son, life was more vivid than it is now. Everything was more distinct. The hours of the day lasted longer. One lived excitedly and dangerously. There was a war on.

Pierre looks ahead at the painting on the wall opposite and wonders if the annual allowance that his mother gives him on the condition that he keeps on good terms with his father is worth it.

"We really lived our life," says Paul.

It's like the electric fixtures in Peregrine's apartment, Pierre meanwhile is reflecting. In Peregrine's apartment, which is a long barn-shaped room on the third floor of a barn-like warehouse off lower Broadway, the main lighting fixture in the ceiling is fitted with a three-way adapter into whose sockets are fitted, in turn, the light bulb, a cord lead-

ing to a two-plate cooking stove and a longer cord leading
to a further three-way adapter which is hooked on to the
wall. The adapter on the wall also has three sockets: one
for an electric razor, another for a bright lamp which
Peregrine uses when he works at his drawings at night and
the third is a free-lance receptacle for an iron, a coffee-pot,
an electric cork-opener and various other electrical things
which Peregrine uses alternately. When Peregrine first put
up this rigging, it was expected to fuse within a few hours,
a few days, any time; it was predicted that the whole
neighborhood would have a blackout, maybe the whole of
Manhattan, or the Eastern Seaboard. But more than two
years have passed and Peregrine's fuse has not blown. It
must happen any time, any moment, thinks Pierre. Perhaps
it is happening now. My father and mother, and the rest of
us, will blow a fuse and the current will stop flowing, thank
God. Useful as it is, it's all too precarious. I'll get my vital
juice from some other source.

His father says, "You don't seem to take in how real it
all was. And now it's caught up on me again, you don't
seem to believe that I'm in danger. You're like your mother,
Pierre, during the war when we were on secret work. She
was careless."

Pierre gets up and bends over the long window seat to
look down at the street. He says, "Do you see that man
going up towards Fifth? Come and look, Father."

Paul joins him, his nose peering forward.

"There," says Pierre, "the man in the light suit just now
passing the pharmacy, there."

"Yes, why?" says the father.

The stared-at man stops at the corner and turns his head
for a meaningless moment to look across to Pierre's building
as people generally do, as it were obligingly, when picked

on by chance to be looked at from afar. Pierre says, "He's there every night. Usually he stands on the corner for a while then walks back up the street. He's watching the entrance." It is all just a fabrication, but in Pierre's ears it sounds better than his father's kind of truth.

"My God!" says his father, still watching the corner where the man has disappeared.

"Did you recognise him? You know his face?" says the tall son who still holds up the edge of the nylon curtain somewhat sweetly between his thumb and his index finger.

"No," says Paul. "Drop the curtain," he says. "He'll know we've seen him."

Pierre lets it fall from his fingers and pats the curtain into place like a devoted housewife.

"This is serious," says Paul.

The son sits down and looks at his watch. "Yes, really," he says. A police siren swoops past their hearing like a primitive bird and wails on the wing far into the traffic.

"What kind of a daughter are you?" Paul says. "Just what kind of a daughter?"

Katerina says, "I did you credit at school. What did you do for me that's so special?"

"I caused you," says her father.

"Not all by yourself." She smiles with her white teeth seeming to leap from her sun tan.

"I always took the initiative with your mother."

"Well," she says, "that is an interesting piece of data."

"Data is plural. Datum is the singular. I don't know how the hell you did well at school. You don't know a thing."

"You'd be surprised, Pa," says Katerina. "You really would."

She had been lying in bed listening to the church bells

and the air conditioner when her father arrived. Her apartment is, for the present, at East Sixty-fourth Street off Madison Avenue.

When he has gone she writes a letter to her mother asking for money. After some thought she addresses the envelope to Mrs. Paul Hazlett, H.C.F. The letters stand for Highest Common Factor. Katerina feels her mother might ponder as to their significance and so be moved to read the letter. Katerina delivers it herself later in the day, slipping it into her parents' mailbox on the ground floor, there by the East River where they live.

Chapter Three

It is wintertime in Elsa Hazlett's apartment; the rushing summer purr of the air conditioner has ceased; the air quivers with central heating that cannot be turned off very far, and which is augmented by heat from the flats above and below and in the north flank.

"Garven?—Who is Garven?" says Princess Xavier.

"My Guidance Director," Elsa says.

"Liberate yourself from all such people," says the Princess, gathering together her large-lady folds.

"You aren't going yet?—Stay awhile," Elsa says.

The Princess murmurs, while she settles herself back among the cushions, "I have to get home to my mulberries." She says, "I once was in the toils of a priest, my dear Elsa. I liberated myself from him forty years ago and I never regretted it. The first week and the fourth week that I refused him the door were the worst. He had been my anchor and when I gave up this man I felt like a little boat tossing on the great sea of life. But I found my course— I have never regretted cutting loose from that priest." She leans back, puffing her sails like a very big ship, so that one can well believe what she has said.

"Oh, Garven has no religion," Elsa says, "he's not a priest."

"Religion makes no difference," the Princess says. "You should never take guidance from one man only. From many men, many women, yes, by watching them and hearing, and finally consulting with yourself. It's the only way. Life should be one's Guidance Director."

"Oh, Garven amuses me," Elsa says.

"If you enjoy going to visit him then the more reason that you should give him up. You will miss him, and the more you miss him the stronger you will be. Guidance Director! You're better off with your window-thing."

Elsa laughs and goes over to the window, looking out. She says, "It keeps me free," leaving a doubt whether she is referring to Garven or to the window-thing.

But Princess Xavier is not about to be perplexed on any point whatsoever. She is now interested in something else, far away in her thoughts, probably Long Island where her farm of sheep and silkworms will be shivering for want of her presence and, of course, the cold. She opens one of the folds, revealing a pink bulge of bosom. She puts her hand within the crease; her eggs are safe. She is in the habit of keeping the eggs of her silkworms warm between and under her folds of breasts; she also takes new-born lambs to her huge ancestral bed, laying them at her feet early in the cold springtime, and she does many such things. She now folds herself back into her coverings and starts the process of rising from the sofa.

Elsa says, "Paul will be in soon. Can't you wait half an hour and have a drink? He always hates to miss you, Poppy love."

The Princess waddles respectfully round Elsa's shadow to avoid treading on it as it falls across the grand piano and on to the floor like a webby grey cashmere shawl that has been left to trail and gather dust untouched for a hundred years. The Princess says, "Next week I can stay longer, and then go on to the opera from here. Today I have to go early—Francesca is away and I have to see what they are up to, one can't trust them, they . . ." She kisses Elsa, and is seen into the lift by both Elsa and her maid, while she is still explaining the difficulties attaching to her farm. At an earlier time in her life she had spent her days pining and striving for a moderately slim appearance; she had been enterprising in her travels and at last she had married an aged Russian exile who had just lost his job as a pianist in a nightclub in Paris. She took him to London and started an employment agency specialising in foreign exiles, placing her clients wherever an alien tongue or an exotic skill was needed.

After this marriage the Princess made herself fat and fatter, until, ten years later at the time of Prince Xavier's funeral, she had become grand and large, loving all, and much beloved. She had been a foundling Miss Copplestone from New Zealand, and might easily have taken a wrong safe turn, ending up as a saggy supervisor at the telephone exchange. Elsa had never known her differently, having met the Princess when she was already grand-mannered, large and free, even as far back as 1944, there in the world of wartime secrets.

"He's come back," says Paul. "He's back."

Elsa says, "Now, now. You know he isn't Kiel, so what does it matter to you if he's back?"

"I'm convinced it's Kiel without any doubt. And he's back in New York. He's back in the shoe store. He really is Kiel, after all."

"He is too young to be Kiel. You agreed with Garven that people grow older. He's like what Kiel was away back in the war, but Kiel now would be very different even if he hadn't died in prison, which he did."

"When I saw him again today I knew," says Paul, "that it was Kiel. He must have had some rejuvenating treatment."

"Talk to Garven," says Elsa, "don't talk to me. I had enough of this Kiel last summer. All summer you were on about Kiel."

"You saw him first."

"Well, you saw him second. If he was Kiel he would have aged a bit like you," she says.

Paul says, "You didn't say that when you first saw him in the shoe store. You said—"

"It was an illusion like any other illusion," she says, her shadow falling in the wrong unnatural direction, "so I don't know why you bring it up again. The man's not Kiel. So I don't know why you bother. The man can't be Kiel, he's young enough to be Kiel's son. So I don't know why you jumble the facts. All over the place, you tumble."

"You think of everything, my dear, until you think of something else." He speaks softly as if she is becoming dangerous, as indeed she is when she speaks like this.

"Well maybe you don't jumble," she says with suicidal mirth, "I take it back. Cheer up, I'm going to bed."

"No, it's mistake a face that I don't do." He speaks to soothe her, but thinks, Why don't I leave her? Today she's bubbling with hilarity, tomorrow she'll be brooding again. Next week, hysterical gaiety. He says, "Did you see Garven today?"

"Yes, do you know he's starting an institute, The Institute of Guidance. He's the Guidance Director. His own title." She leaves the room, trailing her shadow at the wrong angle, like the train of an antique ball-dress. She is laughing rather fearfully all along the corridor and even when she has shut the door of her room she continues to laugh; her laughter comes straight to his ear as if she commands the air he breathes.

Here he is with the colour photograph in his hand and here, again, he holds the negative up to the light. Katerina, still at school; Pierre, a first-year student; Paul himself in his tennis clothes, shorter than his son, smiling in profile; and Elsa, blonde with the parting of her hair showing dark, trim in her white shorts. Elsa's shadow falls brown in the photograph, grey-white in the negative; it crosses his shadow and the children's as if to conceal them with one sharp diagonal line. Elsa had laughed at the photograph when she first saw it; the children had said nothing about the shadow, they never seemed to notice anything. Only Pierre had said, "The Princess always takes photos out of focus; what a waste!"

"Mother is no fool," says Pierre. "Mother is intelligent. More than one can possibly calculate, she's intelligent, it gives one a jolt sometimes."

The father feels a sudden panic because it is infinitely easier for a man to leave a beautiful woman, to walk out and leave her, and be free, than to leave a woman of intelligence beyond his calculation and her own grasp. "No," Paul shouts. "She's crazy. I have to think for her, I have to do her thinking all the time."

"All right, Father. All right."

"She's cunning, that's all. When she wants to be."

"I went back to the shoe store today, Poppy," Elsa says to the Princess. "I bought some boots," Elsa says, "fur-lined, that I don't need, Poppy, because I wanted to have another look. The other day I bought these shoes I'm wear-ing—do you like them? He's there. He looks like Kiel, too young. Could he be Kiel's son, do you think?"

"He's Kiel," says Poppy. "Kiel with a face-lift. When I went to the store I looked close, my dear, and I saw it was truly Kiel. After all, he was very young when we knew him during the war; very young. He must have had his face lifted, it looks quite stretched at the eyes. You go again and look close, Elsa. You look close. He's stiff at the waist. I bought a pair of evening shoes to be sent C.O.D. but naturally I gave a false name and address. I've got five pairs of evening shoes already. What do I want with more? I rarely wear them. Did you notice how he bends, stiff at the knees, thick at the waist, like a prisoner of long years. As he *has been*."

"I know he's Kiel," Elsa says. "I know it very well. I wish you would be more obliging, Poppy, and pretend he's someone else. If Paul could be induced to believe this man's somebody else, then he will become sombody else. It's a matter of persevering in a pretence. Paul must be persuaded against his judgment and persevere against it."

"If you weren't an old friend of mine that I know so well I'd think you were sinister," states the Princess agree-ably, as she takes out her powder compact and looks closely at her face as if to verify to herself that she has uttered no lie. She looks back at Elsa again and says, "Ut-terly unscrupulous." She then pats her nose and jowls with creamy powder, while the central heating quivers in the air and, outside the window, snowflakes begin to fold into clouds descending as they have done, off and on, for so many weeks.

Neat, orderly Delia, who has been the Hazletts' daily maid for more than six years, comes in, looking as usual, to collect the tea-tray and get the washing-up done before going home. She rarely speaks except to say good afternoon and good-bye now. She came originally from Puerto Rico with her sister, married a Puerto Rican night porter, and now lives in the Bronx, returning to Puerto Rico every two years at Christmastime with her husband, their suitcase and their twin daughters. This being a Thursday, Delia has had her shiny hair done before coming to work, because Thursday is her husband's night off.

"Your hair looks very good, Delia," Princess Xavier says as the young woman bends over the tray and picks it up. Delia then stands up straight, holding the tray at a little distance from her waist in a manner unusual to her. She waits in this position for a little moment, then spreading her fingers she lets the tray drop from her hands.

"Oh!" says the Princess.

Elsa and the maid say nothing. The three women stare at the wreckage on the carpet, at the silver teapot on its side oozing leafy tea, the cream crawling its way among the jagged fragments of Elsa's turn-of-the-century Coalport china, the petits fours and scones from Schrafft's, Fifth Avenue, and the pineapple preserves from Charles, Madison Avenue; they stare at the sugar cubes scattered over the carpet like children's discarded playing-blocks seen from a far height. Then Delia says, "You people are lousy. Katerina and Mr. Hazlett is lousy, your son Pierre is lousy, my husband is lousy and the kids is just so lousy as well, this rat in my home is lousy and his lice is lousy."

"She has never said such a thing before," Elsa says.

Delia then runs to the window and wrenches at the latch-handle, scratching with her little fingers and freshly painted nails to get it open; it is stiff, for it has not been opened for the past eight weeks.

"She's going to throw herself out!" says the Princess, rolling like a ship to rise to her feet.

"Don't open the window, Delia," says Elsa, "because it upsets the central heating. One should never open the windows when the central heating or the air conditioners are turned on, as it creates an atmospheric imbalance. If the room is too hot, Delia, you can turn down the heating by means of that tap by the side of the radiator, you turn it to the right. If that fails to reduce the heat—"

"Elsa," says the Princess, "come and hold her!"

Delia is trying all the windows in turn and now she is fighting off Princess Xavier while attempting to reach the east window behind Elsa which looks out on the dark day-light full of snow, a swirling grey spotted-muslin veil, be-yond which, only by faith and experience can you know, stands the sky over the East River.

In the end they get the girl to sit down, then to lie down on the sofa, then to sip water, while Elsa telephones to Garven. Delia says nothing but just lies and looks sourly about the room with the corners of her mouth turned down ex-ceedingly, distorting her usual prettiness, in an expression of entire disgust. The Princess sits by her side making re-marks intended to soothe, such as "We all feel that way sometimes," and "It will all have blown over by tomor-row." So she must have sat many hours at her desk of Prin-cess Xavier's Agency in Bayswater, dispensing into the nerve-racked ears of Europe's refugees sentiments which were all the more hypnotic in effect for having been unintelligible.

Elsa goes and brings a brush and pan, and starts sweeping up the mess on the carpet, her shadow weaving as she kneels. "When Garven arrives," she says, as she sweeps and gathers-up, "he will say to Delia, 'What's your problem?' Those will be his words, I would place a bet on it. So she will have to think of a problem whether she has one or not."

Delia does not respond, even with a lowering of her frown or a lifting of it. The Princess says, "I dare say the poor girl does have a private problem."

"Not necessarily," Elsa says. "It doesn't follow, really, at all, that she has a problem."

The key in the lock away in the distance of the front door lets in Paul. The Princess gazes down at Delia, settling herself so as to present a tableau for Paul's appearance in the room. Elsa stands up, brush and pan in hand; she looks out of the window at the obscure snow-sky, giggles, and again kneels to her sweeping-up. Paul enters and stops in the doorway: "What have you been doing, Elsa?"

"I knifed the girl," Elsa says.

"Nothing of the kind," says the Princess. "Keep quiet, Paul. Delia has had a nervous crisis."

"Lousy people," Delia says, breathing heavily.

"Just lie quiet, my dear," the Princess says. "Mrs. Hazlett's own doctor is on his way to see you."

"I feel bad," Delia shouts. "Lousy, like my head falls off."

"Let her go home," says Paul. He moves closer and is staring at his wife, who, kneeling with her back to him, is now attempting to remove the effects of cream from the carpet.

"Give her some water," Paul says, still staring down towards his wife's behind.

"I don't want no more lousy water," Delia screams.

The Princess grips Delia's wrists in her expert way. "Paul, don't just stand there," she says, "staring like that. It isn't Elsa's fault. Get some brandy for the poor girl. She's going to have another brainstorm."

Delia, however, for a while subsides. Paul says, "Elsa, there's something on the soles of your shoes."

Elsa goes on doing what she is doing.

"Did you know," says Paul, "that there's writing on the soles of your shoes?"

Elsa giggles.

"Take them off. Give them to me."

The doorbell rings. "That's Garven," says Elsa. "Go and let him in."

But Paul has got down on the floor beside her. He grasps an ankle, which overturns her. Then he starts to pull off her shoes. They are fixed by straps and will not wrench off. Elsa kicks mightily, the shadows of her legs waving in his face, whereas by right they should be waving in her own.

"Lousy devils!" Delia shouts, as she has never done on any other day in all her six years with them. "Answer that door! I got to talk to a doctor." The bell pierces long.

The Princess heaves to her feet and hugging her folds paddles off to admit Garven with whom she returns, whispering heavily to him.

Paul has got one of Elsa's shoes off and is trying to unstrap the other while Elsa, lying back among the broken china, tugs his black and grey hair. Delia, supine on the sofa, growls through her lower teeth.

Garven surveys the scene with satisfied disapproval.

"What's your problem?" he says.

Elsa looks over to the east window and starts to laugh. Paul gets the other shoe off.

"Take it easy," says Garven, helping Elsa to her feet. He goes over to Paul, who is examining the soles of the shoes under the light of a lamp. Garven murmurs, "Was she kicking? Did she have a fit?"

Paul does not look up. "The maid fainted or something. Go and do something for her."

"I have to know," Garven says, "what exactly Elsa has done. We may have reached a crisis."

Elsa brushes past them, in her stocking feet, carrying away the tea-tray of wreckage in a business-like manner.

Garven goes over to the maid, whose eyes are now shut, her hand held by the Princess.

"Now what's the trouble?" says Garven with a policeman's authority.

"The girl's had a fit of nerves. She dropped the tray. Elsa was sitting over there quite calmly."

"It's too hot in here," Garven says. "Stifling. Can't you turn down your heating?" He feels the girl's head, but his eyes are on Paul. "Elsa called me," he says.

"I know," says the Princess. "Paul arrived later, didn't you, Paul?"

"This is in code," says Paul, coming over to the Princess with the under-soles of Elsa's shoes held out to her. "It's a means of communication for secret work. You mark a pair of new shoes in a certain way, practically invisible until they are worn in the street. When the soles get dirty the markings show up and you can read the message. There's writing on the soles of these shoes—can you read it?"

Three rows of faint scratchings can be seen on each of the under-soles. The Princess says, "My spectacles are in my bag, Paul. Let Mr. Garven deal with this poor girl."

Garven is over by the north window where the main radiator is. He is trying to turn off the control knob which is already turned off as far as it will go. He lays his hands on the very hot radiator. "These old apartment houses," he says.

"Mr. Garven," says the Princess, rolling big eyes to indicate Delia and the fact that his duty lies there.

"Always too hot," Garven says, frantically, now pulling at the knot of his tie, and anxiously looking around the room for guidance. Paul stands peering at the soles of the shoes.

"My name," Garven informs the Princess, "is Bey, spelt B—E—Y. My surname."

"Oh, I thought you were a Mr. Garven. Garven is your Christian name, is it?"

"My prename. These goddam old apartments—"

"Lousy language, your doctor," shouts Delia, who now starts up from the sofa. "All lousy, here. What you done for Mrs. Hazlett all the lousy money she spent on you? What you ever done for her?"

After which Delia runs out of the room and her footsteps can be heard along the corridor to the kitchen. From there her voice can still be heard, but not her words.

"New York is changing," says Princess Xavier.

"What did you want to bring me here for?" Garven says. "This is a madhouse. Why me?"

"Have you got your reading spectacles, Poppy?" says Paul impatiently, indicating her bag with one of the shoes. "This is important," he says. "I want you to see."

The front doorbell rings. Garven looks at his watch, takes out his handkerchief and pats his forehead. The front door can be heard being opened. "A madhouse," Garven says and looks again at his watch.

The Princess fetches her glasses out of her bag and takes her time to put them on properly. "Let us see," she says soothingly. "Sit down, Mr. Garven, there's no hurry."

"I'm a busy man," Garven says.

The Princess is peering closely at one of the shoes. Then she holds it at arm's length, to study it. She says to Garven, "Now I must concentrate on this. Sit down. Elsa has your Institute of Guidance at heart. Be patient."

Whereupon Garven sits down.

"I see," says the Princess, "the words, 'Melinda's, New York, Chicago,' which is only the name of the store." She looks towards the door of the room. "Isn't that Katerina I hear?" she says. "Katerina must have stopped by. How nice."

"And underneath?" Paul says. "Below that, what do you see?"

"I can't make it out. Impossible," says the Princess. "Elsa will have to wear them some more, then one will be able to see more clearly. If I were you, Paul, I shouldn't worry." She turns to Garven with an approving smile, apparently because he has been good and sat down when told. And as if to humour him further she loosens the clasp of her shawls. "Yes, it really is very very hot in here," she says, exposing a large expanse of flesh under her low-cut beady afternoon dress.

Katerina comes in with her mother. Delia, growling and dressed for the street, follows.

Garven screams. His eyes are on the Princess's bosom.

He screams. Under the protective folds of her breasts the Princess, this very morning, has concealed for warmth and fear of the frost a precious new consignment of mulberry leaves bearing numerous eggs of silkworms. These have hatched in the heat. The worms themselves now celebrate life by wriggling upon Princess Xavier's breast and causing Garven to scream.

"Lousy doctor," shouts Delia. "I go home now thank you very much." She leaves with a long, loud run and a crash of the front door.

"Katerina, my dear," says the Princess, "fetch me a paper bag. My worms!"

"Don't panic," says Garven to Paul. "Don't panic," he says to Elsa.

Katerina takes a small packet of face tissues from her bag and tosses them on to the Princess's lap. "Wipe them off with these," she says. "Whatever's wrong?—Did you catch some complaint?"

"My little worms," says the Princess, carefully extricating the mulberry leaves from under her lapping breasts, and delicately picking the worms from her skin. She wraps them carefully in the leaves and face tissues and then, after a little hesitation, places them inside her gloves, which she arranges tenderly in her handbag.

Elsa goes to her chair by the east window. "It's stopped snowing," she says.

"Elsa," Paul says. "Elsa—I'm your husband and I'm asking you. What's written on those shoes?"

"Don't panic," says Garven.

"Little things, prematurely born," says the Princess.

"What do you know?" Katerina says, "what do you know— The Pope is going to abolish the colour red for Cardinals."

Her father says, "Katerina, there are messages in code from Kiel on these shoes. Will you be serious for once? Will you think of me for one minute? What kind of daughter are you?"

"I found out something about Kiel for you," she says. "My God, I did! I dated him twice. He's got the clap. I know, because he's given it to me. Now I need treatment quick and I need some money for it. Don't panic."

"Mr. Garven," says the Princess. "Take Miss Hazlett immediately to the hospital. She must not drink from cups that anyone else is going to use."

"It isn't my field," Garven says, "but I'd be happy to recommend—"

"I don't believe her," says Paul. "I don't believe a word she says."

"Elsa!" says Garven. "What's going on here?"

"Get a doctor for Katerina if she needs one," says Elsa, waving her arm in large dismissal.

Garven gives another sort of cry, not a scream, but a deep and chesty sound as if he were groaning from a thousand miles away. He stands up and walks backwards. "There's something wrong with your shadow," he says. "It's falling in the wrong direction." She moves her arm again, waving merrily. He stops walking backwards and looks at the dancing shadow. "Things had to come to a head as I told you, Elsa. This is a major event in your case history. You've externalised."

"Nonsense," says the Princess as she wraps herself up again. "There's nothing new about Elsa's symptom. A discerning healer would have noticed long before this. She's had it for years."

Katerina says, "It even shows in photographs."

"Quiet, quiet," breathes Paul to his daughter. "Don't

bandy these factors about. Have you no respect for your family? You never told me before that you even noticed your mother's disability. Now you come here and open your mouth in front of everyone. Can't you keep a thing to yourself?"

"Yes," she says. "I didn't breathe a word about Ma's shadow to Kiel."

"You saw Kiel?—You did see Kiel?" he says.

"He calls himself Mueller," says Katerina.

"Shadows," says Garven, looking round the room. "Hysteria. Worms. You've externalised, Elsa."

"Externalised what?" she says.

"Your problem." Her Guidance Director looks at her with the anticipation of a fortune to be cultivated and reaped. "A rare if not unique occurrence—a case of externalisation. Probably total."

"She could go in a circus," Katerina says.

"I have to get a new maid," Elsa says. "How do I start?"

Chapter Four

"It gives me the creeps," says Paul, "to have that psycho-analyst waiting on me at table and brushing my suit in the morning. I don't know how you can stand it."

"Delia was so marvellous," Elsa says. "A pity she broke down like that."

"Well, get another girl. Get another girl. This is un-wholesome."

"I can't find a girl. Garven is very willing. He'll do any-thing for us so long as he gets material for his book about my case."

"Then we'll all be exposed in public. He'll make a for-tune and we'll be ruined. Haven't you any foresight?"

Elsa laughs. "He hasn't got his material yet. He's look-ing for the cause, and all I'm giving him are effects. It's lovely." She goes over to the window and looks out, smil-ing.

There is the sound of a key in the door, distantly, along the passage.

"There he is," Paul says. "Here he comes. You can't open your mouth in front of him."

"One can always speak French in front of the servants."

"Do you think he doesn't know French?" Paul says.

"Oh, I don't know about that," says Elsa. "I was only thinking of some way of putting him in his place. What does it matter if he understands what we say, since we never say anything that matters?"

Garven puts his head round the door of the drawing-room and looks at them both in a worried sort of way. "I had a dental appointment," he says. "Did you want anything?"

"Ice," Paul says.

Elsa says, "Would you feel very offended, Garven, if my husband and I conversed in French when you are present in the room?"

"Why?" says Garven.

"In many societies," Elsa says, "it's still usual to speak French in front of servants and young children."

"Elsa!" says Paul.

"Why French?" says Garven.

"Elsa," says Paul. "You're going too far."

"I'm not up in French," says Garven.

"Mr. Hazlett wants you to quit, Garven. If we speak French will you quit?"

"No," says Garven.

"You see?" Elsa says, swaying ostentatiously from the window to the sofa, her shadow waving with her. "You see? He's got future plans for his thesis and his career."

"When I'm through with this job I'll let you know," says Garven, disappearing, so that only his footsteps can be heard receding along the hall towards the kitchen. Presently comes the clink of ice.

"Poor fellow!" says Paul.

The telephone rings.

"That's Pierre," says his mother. "I know his ring. Answer it."

"Hallo," says Paul into the receiver.

"Is everything all right?" says Pierre's voice.

"What do you mean, 'Is everything all right?'" says Paul, looking at Elsa while he repeats his son's question, as it may be for her to hear.

"Is it a good day or a bad day?"

"What do you mean, 'Is it a good day or a bad day?'"

"Tell him it's a good day," says Elsa. "He means me. Tell him it's one of my good days. Come along, tell him."

But Paul's attention is meanwhile eared to the voice at the other end and his free hand stretches forth with a helpless flutter to hush Elsa's talk, like the hand of that King Canute who forbade the sea to advance in order merely to illustrate the futility of the attempt.

"I can't hear what you say," says Paul into the mouthpiece. "Your mother's talking. I can't stand this house any more, this Garven. Are you at home now? I'll be right over."

"Back in 1944 when people were normal and there was a world war on," says Paul to his son, "it was a serious thing to be a spy. Very serious indeed."

"Was it?" says Pierre. "Do you hear that, Peregrine?" he says, addressing his friend who sits shapelessly on the sofa blinking his pinkish eyes, and drinking whisky and soda from a tall fluted glass. "Father says," says Pierre, "that it was a serious thing to be a spy back in the old days."

Paul says to his son's guest, "I was instrumental in sending a spy to prison. He was a German, a very dangerous, wild personality. Of course he was a double agent. Then he got wounded while trying to escape from his prison. He was shot. A few months later we heard that he died of the wounds. But that was a ruse. He didn't die at all. Somebody else must have been substituted for him. I know, because I've seen him in New York."

Peregrine shifts his eyes to tall young Pierre, who is tipping tonic water into his gin with a disdainful backward motion of the wrist and haughty lowered lids, gestures that do not, however, signify anything special. "Is that the guy you just went to check up on in the German prison?" Peregrine says to his friend.

"It is," says Pierre.

Paul looks at the two young men and his thoughts turn panicky: This has all happened a long time ago, he thinks. What is now? Now is never, never. Only then exists. Where shall I turn next? New York is changing. Help me! Help me! He says, "It was a fruitless journey, Pierre."

"Oh, I wouldn't say that," Pierre says. "The truth is always fruitful."

"The truth, yes," says the father. "But you failed to find the truth. The records have been falsified. Kiel is here in New York and he's after me. They always get their revenge."

Peregrine sips his drink and then turns the glass this way and that, as if he too feels that all this palaver has occurred many times before, many times, like the new spring today blowing in on Manhattan from Long Island Sound, making the dust dance on the pavements.

"About this show that Pierre and I are planning to put on at the Very Much Club," he says, "we don't have a lot of time to get started if we want the spring audiences; May, June at the latest. But we can't fail, Mr. Hazlett, that's for sure. It's right for the spring."

But Paul is still in the compound of Intelligence buildings in the spring of 1944. He is twenty-eight. Paul has been back and forward to England since his late school-days, having been sent from Montenegro to his father's English relatives. He studied in Paris, then London. "His intellect has a hundred eyes," his mother wrote to her friends. In fact he has made his way quite well, starting on foreign broadcasts for the B.B.C. Then, since it had come round to wartime, he was sent to the Compound, a secret government department which specialised in propaganda broadcasts to Europe.

"I'm not ambitious," he says to Elsa when he has fallen in love with her. "Not an ambitious man at all." He says this in self-commendation; what he really means is that he is afraid he will not be successful in achieving any ambitions. She is not interested one way or another in his ambitions, being attracted to him in any case more and more, day after day. If he should say he is ambitious for anything whatsoever the word would not mean anything to her. She is twenty-three, and at this time does not cast a shadow at the least angle different from anybody else's within her range of visible light; sunlight and artificial light act on Elsa as they do on everyone else.

The norm in the air about Elsa and Paul is the war with Germany.

At times, when she is not on late duty, Elsa takes the German prisoners for walks in the country within a five-mile radius of the Compound. For various reasons these men, having been taken prisoners of war, have chosen to leave their camps and work for their enemy. What they are engaged with in this particular compound is known as black propaganda and psychological warfare. This is the propagation of the Allied point of view under the guise of the German point of view; it involves a tangled mixture of damaging lies, flattering and plausible truths.

"I think you're out of your element," says Miles Bunting to Elsa. He is a lanky man with a twisted smile, reputed to be the most intelligent member of the Compound. The Compound is reputed to be the most intelligent outfit of the war. The source from which these reputations have arisen will never be found.

"I think you're out of your mind," she says.

"Our war-effort here is extremely valuable," he says.

"Valuable to yourselves," says she.

"No, to the country," he says. And he adds, "We have means of testing the results. These are things you don't know a thing about."

She has said the place is ridiculous. Deep in the heart of it, she is nevertheless deprived of any insight into its doing. It is the policy of the little organisation to tell the workers only what they need to know to perform their individual functions.

Miles Bunting says again, "You're out of your element."

"And you, your mind," she says.

It is true she is out of her element; for one thing she is the only member of the Compound who does not know German. And in a sense it is true he is out of his mind for indulging a desire to confide in her, with hints and references to which she cannot possibly attach a meaning, as if she were a member of the inner circle at the Compound. He has simply overlooked her limited knowledge, drawn by her extreme attractiveness.

Among the women in the house where she is billeted is large Princess Xavier who has already met Paul in London. "Poppy," says Elsa, "would you marry Paul if you were me?"

"I'm not ambitious," Paul says to Elsa when he has fallen in love with her. "Not ambitious at all."

He takes Elsa to London on their fortnightly leave, which they arrange to coincide. They have stayed first at a borrowed flat in Clarges Street, then at the Strand Palace Hotel which is less comfortable since they have to produce their identification cards and ration books, each bearing different names, so that they are obliged to creep in and out of one or the other single room early in the morning, and to tip the floor-page heavily.

Elsa's main job at the Compound consists of taking messages and reports from military Intelligence personnel on a special green telephone used everywhere during the war for secret communications. It is known as a scrambler, because the connection is heavily jammed with jangling caterwauls to protect the conversation against eavesdropping; this harrowing noise all but prevents the speakers from hearing each other, but once the knack is mastered it is easy to hear the voice at the other end giving such information as flight details from newly returned bomber missions, the numbers sent, the numbers lost, the numbers of enemy planes felled. Numbers and numbers over Germany and France. Cities and factories. Pinpoints and numbers piercing the scrambler.

And sometimes in the afternoons she takes the Germans for walks within the five-mile radius of the Compound that is allowed to them. Perhaps it is because she speaks no German that these men tend to say more to her in English than they would do in their own language. It is a common misunderstanding that one who does not know another's mother tongue is assumed to be less intelligent and discerning than he is. In this way, most of the handful of the German prisoners whom Elsa takes for country walks underestimate her wits.

Besides which, they are mostly edgy; whatever the degree of conviction that has led them to work for the enemy, there remains a nagging knowledge that they have deserted their native forces.

Only two amongst them are entirely at ease with themselves: a young dedicated communist and an Austrian count.

And so, before Paul arrives at the Compound and about the time that Miles Bunting is starting loftily to put her at odds, she occupies her bored afternoons by taking them for walks, one by one.

They are walking along the edge of a wood. Rudi is a flat-faced man in his early twenties. He walks with a curious wading motion, with Elsa by his side keeping solemn time while blankly noting him within herself, placing him on record with her in-dwelling daemon. He is gloomy today. The men he is billeted with, the other prisoners of war who are working for the British, are getting on his nerves. He says they had a fight the night before; it all started with one accusing another of leaving a rim round the edge of the bath. He says that anyhow, he is sure to be shot before long. D-Day is coming up, he says. And he waves his hands towards the thick woods to their left and tells her that Hitler's parachutists will soon be filling these woods. He speaks with a sort of bitter, convinced pride like a Judas foretelling hell-fires awaiting him as a boastful proof of his betrayed master's divinity. Elsa tells him to cheer up. She reminds him that only last week he was bubbling with joy to think that the war would soon be over, and he could go down to the beach with his friends at home as he had done before. But he wades on gazing down at the path, depressed. "My family will find that I've been working for the British. Here, we have lard to eat. They have no lard in Germany today. They will say I have done it for lard. They will never have me back." She says, "Oh, you're very erratic." "Erotic?" He brightens with the word, smiling towards her. "*Erratic*," she repeats. He stops and takes his little dictionary from the inside pocket of his saggy tweed jacket and gravely looks up the word.

They are walking along the edge of the wood. This time it is another of the band, Heinz the communist, small and tough, the survivor of a captured U-boat, who shakes hands with himself continually for his decision to work against Hitler and who looks with breezy energy to the inevitable defeat of Germany when he hopes to take up his peacetime job as a waiter in London instead of Hamburg. Heinz the communist and Erich the count are her favorite walking-partners. Some afternoons they walk all three together. The two men practise their English on Elsa. The path by the edge of the wood is narrow, for the fields have been furrowed to the verge because of the war-time need for crops to grow on as many lengths and patches of earth as possible.

They walk through the woods now, these three, talking of their past as if they were middle-aged and not all in their young twenties. The war has given them a past. It will never be the same afterwards. They none of them want it so. Heinz speaks cheerfully of his boyhood in the cold alleys of Berlin. Erich glimpses a rabbit before it bobs into its hole. "If I had a gun I would have shot him for supper," he says. "As a boy I shot rabbits." "I stole rabbits," says Heinz, and goes on to recount, in English that becomes more curiously constructed as his story develops, how adept he was as a boy at slipping dead rabbits off their hooks, where they hung at the doors of big butcher shops, then bearing them to an alley butcher's where he obtained a very small but precious price for them. So they talk of their past, Heinz, with his alley-wits in the hungry back streets, his gang battles with the Hitler Youth and his training as a radio operator in the navy in the early days of the war, gives out his past in a series of pictures, distinct, primitive, undisdainful, without hope, without pain, without any comment but the grin and laugh of a constitutional survivor who has, and always will have, plans for the future.

Erich, whose home is a castle among the mountains of Southern Austria, now occupied by the military, does not seem to care much that it once contained his past life. This past of his still clings about his young personality in bits, as late leaves droop singly from a winter tree; he has shaken off most of it. He was married shortly before the war. It was not a love match. "But," he has once said, "if I find they have killed my wife I shall of course shoot myself." He trudges through the woods with Heinz and Elsa, identifying birds by their calls, naming ferns, examining burrows in the earth and catkins on the trees, about all of which he is explicitly knowledgeable. They trudge through last year's leaves under the spring foliage and speculate as everyone else is doing about the forthcoming D-Day, whether the Allies will attack from North Africa, from Norway or from the Channel. Elsa, too, has brought her past life with her and shares it as casually as she shares the sandwiches of bread, margarine and bits of cold bacon whenever she can scrape these items together from her allotted rations. She brings with her scraps of her life in a family of poor relations in a semi-detached house in Sevenoaks, a tumble-down education at a boarding school where she played lacrosse and the piano. The three laugh often, for they think of things to laugh about and offer them round, one by one, until it is time to return to the village and wait for the official bus at four o'clock which will carry them to the Compound for their work. The villagers stare at them with contempt, not knowing in the least what is going on, but knowing only that their countryside is peppered with Germans and that somehow the authorities permit it.

Only once Elsa and one of her German companions are arrested. A policeman new to these parts hears the foreign accent and demands their identity cards; he is not in the least satisfied. Elsa and her German quietly accept his invitation to the police station. It is a still, sunny afternoon. The sergeant on duty is vaguely aware that foreigners are locally engaged on secret work, but he is taking no chances. Elsa gives a telephone number and the sergeant disappears. She sits quietly with her companion, a middle-aged philosopher from Dresden. They sit for a while under the eyes of the policeman who has brought them in. Then the German starts to protest. He is indignant. His nerves have had enough of policemen, and he has not taken the step of joining with the British in order to find himself once more in the hands of any police whatsoever. "It's all right," Elsa keeps saying. "Don't worry." The sergeant returns, this time rather embarrassed but still not disposed to commit himself to an apology. The young policeman stands guard by the door while the sergeant goes behind a counter and starts writing in a ledger-like book with raised eyebrows to

betoken nonchalance. "To be treated like a pissing schoolboy!" says the German professor. The sergeant writes on,
the policeman stands on, and Elsa continues to reassure her
companion: "They'll come and rescue us in a minute or
two." The Security officer at the Compound turns up by
car within twenty minutes, accompanied by the Chief Con-
stable of the County, formally recognises Elsa and the prisoner and whizzes them off in the car while the sergeant is
still saying, "We can't take any chances you know." The
Security officer mutters all the way to the Compound about
what a raspberry the police are going to get because of this,
a raspberry in these days being already an outdated expression meaning a reprimand. A man less set in his limited
ways than the Security officer would call it a rocket in this
English spring of 1944 when rocket missiles are leaping on
London and the word is one of such that you either have to
bandy it about as a euphemism or sit down, weep and give
up.

They are walking along the path at the edge of the
wood. Helmut has newly arrived at the Compound. He is
called simply Kiel, whereas Claus Kiel is always known as
Claus. Not that either name is the men's own; but both at
the beginning, after they secretly volunteered for separate
batches of the German prisoners of war, and were tested,
and vetted, and eavesdropped upon for months on end,
opted for the cover name of Kiel. Claus Kiel is a gentle, ill-
favoured boy with puny limbs all at odds with each other,
pale, thin and nervous, with a vague and tentative leaning
towards artistic appreciation. In any other fighting nation
but Nazi Germany he would have been rejected for military service and this is plainly why, when the opportunity
arose, he took refuge with the British cause, lest he should

be sent back to Germany when one of the periodic exchanges of prisoners should take place, and so be obliged to engage once more in the physical nightmare of combat.

Helmut Kiel is a different concept altogether. According to Allied information gathered in the course of the months preceding his acceptance for British secret service, he was the wild bad boy of his German training unit.

Helmut Kiel joined the defectors' Compound a few weeks before Paul Hazlett. They have a fight. It starts with an argument over their work, something trivial. The real cause is Elsa. They knock each other about in a field behind the Compound. Not Kiel, but Paul is rebuked, on the grounds that Paul has the unfair advantage over Kiel in that he is not a prisoner of war. The affair is passed off as one of those explosions of nerves that occur in the Compound and in the billets.

In the house where Elsa is quartered she is in trouble. The room she occupies is large enough for two beds but she has refused to share the room with another girl. The elderly women who administer these affairs send for her to come to them in their bottle-green office in London. Greying print dresses hang over their drooping figures. They hunch over their desks. One of them tells her, "It's the regulations that girls under thirty have to share a room. Only women of thirty and more are entitled to a room to themselves."

"I need a room to myself," Elsa says. "I won't share."

"There's a war on," one of these draped billet-administrators reminds her in a voice which cracks like a scratchy gramophone needle on an old record.

"But," says Elsa, "it wouldn't be possible for me to share with another girl. It wouldn't be comfortable for the other girl. I see things."

"What?" says the one. "You what?" says the other.

Elsa swings her bare brown legs in the chair. Her clothing coupons do not run to stockings for every-day occasions.

"Well, yes," she says, "I am really a bit uncanny. I have supernatural communications." There is a large round government clock stuck up on the wall, its size hideously magnifying the importance of working hours and seconds. Underneath it, a poster, unaccountably weather-beaten, bears the motto CARELESS TALK COSTS LIVES.

The billet-administrators, who have been up to now, to all appearances, identical, invisibly separate themselves, hearing Elsa's explanation, into senior official and less senior. The senior draws Elsa's file towards her, puts on her reading spectacles, and begins to read the details set forth on the first folio, while her lesser-paid colleague cranes forth her head over the desk and says probingly to Elsa, as if interviewing her for her qualifications in the field of aberrant sex, "Do you use an instrument?"

"No, it isn't necessary," says Elsa, "for spiritual communication." She is looking at the large clock-face and noting that she is late for her appointment with Paul. This is their second leave together in London. She says, "I can't wait too long. I must go, I'm afraid. I'm on leave, actually, you know."

Nobody is put to share her room. Elsa is rather disliked on this account, her only friend being Poppy Xavier, who has the best room in the house to herself as a matter of course.

"*Peter Pan*," says Paul Hazlett to his son. "Is that what you called me over here to discuss?"

"You were not called over by me. You said you wanted to come."

"Garven is getting me down. A psychoanalyst working in my house as a butler. He's determined to document her case history. Our lives will be an open book."

"Why don't you go away?"

"I can't leave your mother. What are you saying? What are you telling me?"

"Walk out. Leave her alone with Garven."

"Is that what she wants?"

"I wouldn't be surprised."

"I couldn't do a thing like that," says Paul. "I couldn't walk out and leave your mother in difficulties. She was in difficulties with Kiel. Now if she gets in difficulties with Garven—"

"Something new," Pierre says.

"What?"

"Her difficulty with Kiel," Pierre says. "You never said before she was in difficulty with him."

"Well she was. She's a difficult woman, and he was a spy. Do you know what he did? He got himself taken prisoner by us, then he got himself a job with our Intelligence unit on the pretext of being anti-Nazi. After he'd been broadcasting for our outfit six months he picked a fight and got himself sent back to the prison camp. Three days later he went on the air in a prisoners of war exchange-of-greetings programme. He sent a simple message to his mother and sister. But his voice was recognisable, you see. He'd been broadcasting for us. We were supposed to be an authentic underground German station. His voice was recognisable. We weren't sure, but it was definitely possible that Kiel did it deliberately to betray our identity."

"Why was he allowed to do it? Wasn't there any security?"

Paul says, "You might well ask. Our security slipped up."

"Well, it was a long time ago," Pierre is saying as he flicks through the bound pages of a script lying on his knee. "Your mother was in difficulty with Kiel. She was suspected of having an affair with him. I had to get her out of that difficulty. And I did."

"You put Kiel in jail after the war?"

"I was instrumental. Everyone else thought he was just a wild boy. But he was an agent, all right. I tracked him down as an S.S. man. He'd been in the S.S. all along. He started operating in the East after the war. I got him out of there. He did some damage but we got him in the end."

"Well he's dead now," Pierre is saying. "Poor old Kiel."

"He's here in New York," says Paul.

"No, he isn't," says Pierre.

"Princess Xavier thinks so."

"Does she? I thought she didn't."

"Sometimes she does," says the father, "and sometimes she doesn't. You can't trust women."

"Mother doesn't think it's Kiel. She thinks he looks too young."

"It depends," says Paul, "what she's feeling like. One week she'll say yes and the next week she'll say no. I say yes."

"I say no," says Pierre. "I went and established it. He died in jail."

"The records are wrong. He must have had a body substituted for his."

"Why don't you forget it?" says Pierre.

"My life's in danger," says Paul. "Messages on the soles of shoes."

"Katerina says he's a shoe-store man, nothing more."

"Your sister Katerina's a liar. She hasn't been near him."

"She says she has."

"Yes, she says. She's no good. She says anything."

"What does it matter? Spies don't matter any more," Pierre says. "There isn't any war and peace any more, no good and evil, no communism, no capitalism, no fascism. There's only one area of conflict left and that's between absurdity and intelligence."

"Oh, for God's sake," says the father. "What are you trying to do to me, you and Katerina together? My life's in danger. Look at your mother, she's in difficulties."

"Her shadow falls the way it wants," Pierre says.

"Stop!" says Paul. "I won't hear it!"

"You think I haven't noticed it?"

"You must be crazy," says Paul. His throat beats with a throbbing that reaches his ears; "Help me, help me," cries the throb.

"*Peter Pan*," says Pierre, "is going to be a very big success. We aren't changing a word of it. We have permission to put it on; we have a contract. We didn't tell the J. M. Barrie trustees that everyone who's acting in it is over sixty. The age doesn't come into the contract. They can't stop us. It'll be a riot."

"If we could get rid of Garven," Paul says, "I'd raise the money or the best part of it and help you. It sounds obscene, though."

"*Peter Pan* is a very obscene play. Our presentation will only help to direct attention to that fact," says Pierre, looking cornerwise at his father. "Our talent will reveal the absurdity of the thing. The show will be a success, a big success."

"If we could get rid of Garven," Paul says.

"And Kiel? You still want to get rid of Kiel?" says his son.

"Of course. That's the most urgent factor, Kiel."

"And Garven?"

"Garven has to go."

"Set them one against the other," says the son.

"How?" says the father. "That's what I ask. You think I haven't thought of it?"

"Money," says Pierre, "is how things are done."

"Not everything," says Paul, "that's what you of the younger generation don't realize."

"I'm not of the younger generation," Pierre says. "I'm only younger than you. The younger generation is a whole generation away from mine. Nothing to do with me."

"I have to go," says Paul, clinking the ice at the bottom of his glass, then draining what liquid remains in it. He looks at his very flat gold wrist watch. "I have to go," he says.

"To your analyst," Pierre says.

"What?"

"You have to see your analyst."

"Who told you that?" says Paul.

"The name of my informant," says the son, "is—let me see . . . what was it? . . . the name of my informant . . . the name of . . . the name. The name escapes me."

"Your informant has made a mistake."

"Oh no," says Pierre. "Oh no, nothing escapes my informant."

"What have you heard, what on earth have you heard?" says Paul. "What's this about me and an analyst?"

"Well, of course she's all right. There's no reason why you shouldn't do as you please. Do as you please." Pierre's right hand turns on his wrist permissively while his left hand flicks the neatly bound acting script which lies now on a table by his chair. His long legs sprawl before him. "Rather narrow," he says. He pats the script. "I mean she's rather narrow to look at, I feel. One of those narrow-hipped, narrow-faced women who are just born that way and die that way. The effect is just simply narrow, except from the side where they protrude in a few places, nose, breasts, backside and feet. But her voice is just so awful. How can you stand it, Father? It's so absolutely yak-yak-yak. It's a poor way to spend one's money in my view, but of course that's quite your business. Entirely your business."

Paul is standing now. His eye is on the playscript. His hand goes to the inside pocket of his coat.

"Tell me about your production of *Peter Pan*," says Paul.

"I've told you."

"You need money for it."

"Yes."

"I'll need a few days. Maybe I could give you something in advance, though."

"Right now?"

"Yes, now. You did wrong to trail me. You shouldn't have your father followed."

"I didn't trail you at all. She trailed me. Very badly. She drew herself to my attention, did your narrow, narrow analyst."

"God help me!" says Paul. "Your mother mustn't hear of it."

"That's quite my point," Pierre says.

"It's blackmail, of course," Paul says.

"Everything's blackmail. But in fact it's a good idea,

good business, this production of *Peter Pan*. We're not changing a word. It'll be a riot. Everyone over sixty. That's to say, if possible. We might have to settle for an actress around fifty-four to play Wendy."

"Is this what you brought me over here to tell me?" the father says.

"You suggested coming yourself. It was your idea."

"Sooner or later you would have told me all this."

"Oh, quite soon."

"But I'm sorry I came."

"Want another drink?"

"I need more ice."

Pierre is chucking two little blocks of ice into his father's glass while he says, "Need you call it blackmail, anyway?" The father has not produced any cheque from his pocket. His hand has withdrawn from it, empty.

"I need not call it anything. I don't need to say anything. Islanders don't need to speak to each other for survival. They act in unison. They do it by telepathy."

"We are not islanders here in New York."

"You and your sister never became Americanised in the sense that I was Anglicised."

"You are not very English," says Pierre, "although you may think you are."

"What it boils down to," says Paul, "is that you didn't like that word 'blackmail.' "

"No, it could have been left to telepathy."

"Nevertheless," says Paul, reaching again, really this time, for his cheque book, "I said it, and by God I'm glad I did."

Chapter Five

She stamps her right foot.

"They fit like a glove," the salesman says.

"No, they're a bit large," she says. "When you lose weight as I have, you know, you lose it everywhere. Everything's a bit large."

"You need a smaller size, a half-size smaller, Elsa," says the salesman, walking reflectively round her with his eyes on her feet. "I don't know," he says in his precise foreign voice, "if we have a smaller size in that model. I'll have to see."

She stamps her left foot. "Definitely too big. Boots especially—you know, they slip up and down your leg if they're too big."

"A minute," he says, and goes to the back of the shop. Elsa yawns. A very thin woman with a champagne-coloured head of dead-looking hair and a long, squeezed, but distinguished face comes in and stares around, waiting, it seems, for an assistant. It is the lunch-hour. No assistant appears, although Elsa's man can be heard playing with cardboard boxes somewhere at the back and, from the sound, evidently high up on a ladder.

"He won't be a minute," Elsa tells the woman, and sits down.

The woman sits down, too, and looks at Elsa's shadow, then at her own, then at the other shadows, referring them, too, back to Elsa's.

"Yes," says Elsa.

"What?" says the woman.

"Now you know," Elsa says.

"Excuse me?" says the woman.

"You know it's true, you've seen for yourself," Elsa says. "And now you can button up that common little mutation mink jacket and take yourself back to your office, and put through a call to my husband, and tell him that it's true, he's got a big problem, as he says. I'm tired of seeing you follow me around. You've been shadowing me for three weeks but you're a hopeless shadow."

Her real shadow makes a hopeless gesture in keeping with her real hand. The woman abruptly stands up.

The salesman comes back with two boots, one brown and one red. "Try these for size, Elsa. I'll have to order them in black if you want them in black." Then he notices the other woman, and thinking her fretful, says to her, "Take a seat, madam."

But she goes, buttoning her pale mink jacket, banging the glass door, so that the salesman frowns.

"My husband's analyst," Elsa says. "She's been following me for three weeks."

"She looked upset," says the salesman.

"I told her to clear off," says Elsa. "I was rude."

"Well, now she knows."

"Yes, now she knows. And I dare say she thinks you're Helmut Kiel."

"From all you have told me, Elsa," says the salesman fondly, "I wish I had been that man."

She pulls up the boot, stands, and stamps her left foot.

"Pierre's play is opening at last, next Thursday," she says.

"You must be proud of your son," he says with a correct little bow.

"Well I can't say one way or another till I've seen the reviews."

He giggles, evidently delighted with her ways.

"It should have opened last spring but there was a hitch. My husband didn't finance it enough, so I had to help. The theatre is called the Very Much Club, only it isn't a club, it's a theatre in Greenwich Village, I believe."

"Is it a good play?" says the man, stroking the boots which Elsa has now taken off and handed to him.

"It sounds awful. But it might make money. My son doesn't need money."

"Why don't you just grab your jewellery and run away?" says her friend.

"Why should I take my jewellery?"

"That's what jewellery's for. Every woman grabs her jewellery when she runs away, doesn't she?"

"Only if she has no money. In my case, I'm the one with the money."

"Then go wherever your money is," he says.

"Switzerland," she says. "Switzerland, you know."

She is walking along the Bahnhofstrasse in Zurich, blown by the wind, indifferently passed by the other pedestrians but never jostled. It is so different from Manhattan where one is bumped into and almost placed under arrest by the otherwise occupied passers, and where people rush out of arcades and buildings stripping pieces of paper from candy-bars, then biting the bar and letting fall the paper as they hurry along.

She is standing by the verge of the lake in Zurich, looking back and forth from her reflection in the water to her shadow beside her, smiling at them both. She has lost weight and her shadow is thinner than it was last summer, even allowing for the bulk of her heavy coat and the bulge of the fur collar spreading obliquely behind her, while before her the same shape ripples. "You would have to know a lot about atmospheric physics," she thinks, while a large fat youth tramps methodically past her on his way to work, turning his head towards her with a note-taking interest neither more or less than that of a humble adding-machine.

Now, later in the morning, she is walking once more along the Bahnhofstrasse and glances at her shape in the reflections of the clean shop-windows. At the end she crosses the street, walks back a little way, turns off at a corner and into the hotel where she is staying. It is not quite twelve-thirty. Her friend from the shoe shop is waiting by the door.

"Goodness!" she says. "You really do remind me of that man Kiel I used to know. Just standing there, you looked for a moment so like him."

"Well I wish it was so, in a way, Elsa," he says, "now that you have said what you have said of your youth."

"Let's go to the bar and have a drink," she says, "while we decide where to eat."

Fractional Manhattan is closed for Sunday, but Paul Hazlett has set aside the afternoon, as he frequently does, to work over that anthology, his collection of personal problems old and new.

The apartment on the East River is empty and hot. Paul tries to turn the handles of the radiators in the drawing-room, but they are all swivelled as far to the right as they will go; when they are in this position the heat should be turned off, but, as usual, the old-fashioned radiators burn like kindled stoves to the touch.

The telephone rings and Paul stands up, first looking at it anxiously and then dashing across the floor not to miss it. A voice, when he answers, says, "Call for you from Zurich."

"Paul, it's me," says Elsa's voice.

"What are you doing in Zurich?" he says.

"Getting into bed," she says.

"What's wrong with you?" says Paul.

"Nothing. It's bedtime over here."

"But what are you doing in Zurich?"

"Sleeping with Mr. Mueller."

"You're what?"

"Having an affair with Mr. Mueller."

"Who?"

"Mueller from the shoe shop. The one you call Kiel. He's on vacation here with me."

"Be serious, Elsa."

"I'm sleeping with him to check if he's really Kiel. It's the only way to identify him," she says.

"Then you did sleep with him during the war?" he yells.

"Be careful on the phone, Paul. I slept with him last night. I don't think he's Kiel. He's having a shower at the moment. Maybe I'll call you tomorrow and let you know my final reactions."

"I can have him fired from his job. I can have him arrested as a spy."

"I own the shop," she says. "How can you have him fired? I acquired the shop."

"Did you acquire the State Department, too? He's a spy."

"I was saying, Paul, I don't think he's Helmut Kiel. This one's much too eager. Helmut as a lover was not all that lecherous. His basic approach was different, you had to coax. But this one—"

"What's your hotel, Elsa?"

"The Ritz," she says.

"There isn't a Ritz in Zurich. I'm coming over. I'll make a declaration to the police and I'll bring Garven."

"I think I'll be home day after tomorrow," Elsa says. "As soon as I'm sure of my facts, anyway."

"You believe her?" he says to Katerina on the telephone.

"Well, Pa, it depends if she's given him a nice present or something. He's got plenty of girls."

"I bet he's right here in New York."

"No, they said at the shop he was out of town. On business."

"That's Kiel the spy, all right. Your mother's age."

"I wouldn't say so, not one bit. His name's supposed to be Mueller."

"Did you really date him, Katerina? You had sex with him?"

"Oh, I don't know, Pa. If it wasn't him it was someone else. Mother could be having a game with you, Pa."

"He's having a shower right now, she said."

"It makes quite a picture," Katerina laughs.

"It's her with Kiel in 1944 that makes quite a picture," says Paul. "That's what you don't understand."

"Oh God, what was 1944? It never happened to me," she says.

He is tracking her down on the telephone to Zurich, hotel after hotel, far into the night. At last he talks to her.

"It must be the middle of the night your end," she says, "because it's nearly eight by my watch."

"Where is Kiel?" Paul says. "Pass me Kiel."

"Kiel?"

"Well, Mueller. Mueller, Kiel, I want to speak to him if you please."

"Excuse me," she says, "you've got the wrong number. This is not Ecstasy Farm."

He says, "You called me, Elsa. You told me, Elsa. Take it easy. Try to recollect what you did yesterday."

"I never do today the same as I did yesterday," she says. "Why should I remember?"

"Why are you in Zurich? Come home," he says.

"I'm expecting my breakfast, Paul. They do an American breakfast here. Why should I come home if I can get American breakfast here? Why should I come home if I can get American breakfasts in Switzerland?"

"Is Kiel in the bathroom?"

"Who?"

"Kiel. Mueller, Kiel—is he having another shower?"

"Just hold a minute," says Elsa's voice. "I'll see if there's anybody in the bathroom."

"Elsa!" Paul shouts, but he hears only the sound of the receiver being placed on its side. He waits, watching the seconds-indicator on his watch creep round the dial and creep again. "Elsa!" he shouts. There is a click. "Have you finished speaking?" says the operator from the American end.

"I'm still talking," Paul says. "I'm holding on. My wife—" But he is already cut off.

It takes more than half an hour for Paul to be reconnected. "Can you hold on?" says the European operator.

"I can bear to suffer," Paul says.

"Baby doll," says the operator, "don't aggravate me."

"In the United States of America," says Paul, "we no longer speak that way."

"Hallo," says Elsa. "Allo. Vous êtes en erreur."

"Elsa," he says.

"Oh it's you," she says. "Why are you calling?"

"Who's there with you?" he says.

"You're so tribal," says Elsa.

"Final, did you say?"

"Tribal," she says.

"I don't understand you, Elsa. What do you mean?"

"You can't keep on calling a person from New York early in the morning."

"Who's with you in the room?" Paul says.

"No one," she says. "Why?"

"I just thought there might be," he says patiently, trying not to frighten her. "You did call me yesterday, you know. Don't you remember?"

"What has yesterday got to do with me?" she says.

"Elsa," he says and he looks out of the window at the dark sky above the East River waiting for her to say something else, a something, any little thing to calm his terror. The line is silent. "Elsa, you still there?" he says.

"Yes, what do you want?"

"Be reasonable," he says, and the sound of a police siren wails up First Avenue as he listens to the silent telephone. He says, "Be reasonable. You said the man was with you. Remember you said you were having sex with him to find out if he was Kiel or not. That means you must have had sex with Kiel in 1944, doesn't it?"

"Sex," she says, "is a subject like any other subject. Every bit as interesting as agriculture."

"Have you finished?" says the operator.

"No, we're still talking," Paul says. "This is private." The operator disappears, apparently, with a click. Nevertheless Paul adds, "Please don't interrupt."

"After all," says Elsa, "we're paying for the call, aren't we?"

"I know," Paul says.

"There are English tourists here en route to somewhere," Elsa says. "I passed their table last night and heard one of them saying, 'Jonathan's O-levels. . . .' That was all, but Christ, it made me want to be sick. The English abroad are so awful and they always bring their own life with them. I mean, what's the use of going abroad if you don't get new life from it?"

"I know," says Paul. "When are you coming home?"

"Tomorrow, I think."

"Your experiment's over?"

"Oh yes, the experiment. Well, I can complete it another time."

"Where's Kiel?"

"He's dead, I think. You mean Mueller?"

"Mueller," he says, "Mueller from the shoe store."

"Mueller," she says, "put on his trousers and went away somewhere."

"Be careful on the phone," he says. "I don't know what to believe, Elsa."

"You never did," Elsa says.

"What's the number of your flight, Elsa?"

"I'll call you later," she says. "I'll let you know. Then you can come and meet me, Paul. See you soon. I want to finish breakfast now."

"You won't be coming back with Kiel? Will he be on the plane?"

"Kiel isn't here."

"Don't travel back with him. You'll get yourself in a mess and you'll never be able to shake him off."

"Well, don't come to meet me with Garven."

The operator comes on again. "Still talking?" he says and cuts them off. Paul looks down on the dark and quite dangerous street. "Help me!" cries his mind, with a fear reaching back to the Balkan realities. He looks round the room, panicking for her familiar shadow. He wants her back from that wild Europe, those black forests and gun-metal mountains. Come back to Manhattan the mental clinic, cries his heart, where we analyse and dope the savageries of existence. Come back, it's very centrally heated here, there are shops on the ground floor, you can get anything here that you can get over there and better, money's no object. Why go back all that way where your soul has to fend for itself and you think for yourself in secret while you conform with the others in the open? Come back here to New York the sedative chamber where you don't think at all and you can act as crazily as you like and talk your head off all day, all night.

Come back. He pours himself a whisky, sits down with it, and reflects that after all she isn't in any wild place but in a first-class hotel in Zurich. He takes his drink, switches off the light and goes into a smaller room where papers litter his desk. He switches on the television and gets the late-late show.

Garven, however, bangs on the wall. Paul turns off the television, fetches himself another drink, and goes to bed.

At eleven next morning Paul is sitting dressed by the

telephone in the little room waiting for his next call to Zurich to come through. He has been advised of an hour's delay and only a three-quarters of the hour has materialised. The hand that marks the seconds on his watch looks as if it is knitting a sock, stitch by stitch. Paul lifts the telephone impulsively and dials a number.

A woman's voice answers.

"Annie," he says.

"Hallo, I was just going to call you," she says.

"Why?" says Paul.

"I wanted to say hallo, that's why. Did you hear from her?"

"Yes, I did. She's in Zurich with the shoe salesman. He isn't Kiel, she said. But why should she go to Zurich? She had to sleep with him to find out, that's what she said. It means she cheated me in the past, do you realise? I don't know what to think. Why did she go to Zurich?"

"She would want to contact a new analyst," says Annie. "She would bring him back home with her and start again."

"You shouldn't have got caught following her," says Paul.

"Now, listen," she says.

"I can't," Paul says, "I'm expecting a call from Zurich. I'll talk to you later, Annie." He hangs up, unlocks a drawer in his desk, takes out a set of three keys on a ring and, picking out one of the keys, crosses the room to a glass-fronted bookcase, which he opens. He takes out a large green leather, gold-worked book in fine and shiny condition, closes the bookcase and takes the book under his arm to the desk. He draws out the telephone on its long wire till it extends to a small table by an armchair. Here he sits by the telephone, and opens the book.

It turns out to be a photograph album. The first photographs have a brownish look, and are slightly cracked, as if they belong to the first amateur Kodaks of 1888, although the dresses of some of the people belong to the early nineteen-twenties. All that the discrepancy means, in fact, is that the photographs were taken in a country where everything was thirty years behind the times. It is a family album. The family must have travelled abroad to buy their clothes. The servants, like the camera which has introduced them, are the old-fashioned ones, the women have long skirts, the men whiskers, and stand in a countrified way around the family and their friends. The album is selective in the sense that one child, as Paul turns the pages, recurs in every portrait. Now in a nurse's arms, now with a group of tennis-playing uncles and lipsticked aunts, now alone, holding a tennis racket. Me, thinks Paul, when I was eight months, me when I was nine, underexposed.

It is the next morning and he has failed to locate her. She has not telephoned from Zurich to tell him her flight number. It is seven-thirty when he wakes up in his restless bed. Garven is still asleep; he has made no pretence of being a manservant all during Elsa's absence. He comes and goes, he sleeps late or early as he pleases, pushing the coffee-pot around the kitchen and clattering his breakfast cup as if he owned the place. Paul tries not to coincide with him.

He reaches for the phone, puts in a call to Elsa's hotel in Zurich, jumps out of bed and hastens to his bathroom. Paul shaves and listens for the phone while silence continues to break from Garven's bedroom. He thinks ahead to her arrival at the airport, her fuss with the porter and her luggage, while he waits at the door beyond the customs tables. She

will have to tip the porter very quickly at the point between the luggage reception and the customs. If you want
to tip me, ma'am, tip me now, the porter will say, just as he
is about to wheel forward the piled-up trolley. Elsa will
slip the note into his hand which is already on the trolley
handle. The hand opens and closes and the porter murmurs,
"Ain't allowed," cheerfully pressing on, with the passenger
following the luggage at the trot.

Paul thinks ahead, with his ears open for the ring of the
phone. She should arrive some time around eight tonight.
I'll watch for her flight number on the board, then stand
by the arrivals gate, watching her, busy in her fur coat,
through the customs, showing and explaining and ingratiat-
ing herself most suspiciously with the customs officers. Paul
dresses and goes to make coffee.

A key in the front door. Garven, he thinks. Not in his
room at all, no wonder he was quiet. At that moment he
hears Garven's bedroom radio begin to pour forth the
morning's news. The step in the hall must be that of an in-
truder. It had to happen, Paul thinks, it's happened to
everyone else. He hears a few more steps along the corridor
and he hears Elsa at the door of her bedroom. "Paul," she
says. "The hall porter's bringing up my luggage. Let him
in."

"Why didn't you call me?" Paul says, rushing out of the
kitchen. He kisses her in greeting and shouts, "You damn
bitch, I was waiting up all night to hear the flight number."

"You haven't been to bed?" she says.

"Yes, well I went to bed. But you said, 'I'll call and let
you know the flight number and the arrival time.' I would
have met you."

"Yes," she says, throwing her coat on the bed while her

shadow, regardless of the morning sunlight in front of her, makes the same gesture, hanging a moment from her raised arm like a raglan sleeve. Dust motes dance in the light and her shadow falls casually at a different tangent across the bed like the flung coat. There is a ring at the service door and Garven can be heard plopping in his bedroom slippers along the corridor towards it.

Elsa says, "My room needs an airing."

"We weren't prepared for you," Paul says. "Why didn't you let me know the flight number?"

"Not again," she says. "Never again." She goes to open wide her hanging cupboard, making it ready to receive her clothes. She says, "Remember the last time you met me at Kennedy?"

"The last time?" He makes an effort of memory with his forehead, his eyes go absent, all his energy concentrates on his forehead. He frowns and looks towards her for help. "What happened the last time? So many meetings at airports. When was the last time at Kennedy?"

She is saying, "I'm going to have coffee. Then I'm going to have a bath and change. I slept on the plane, all the way. I'm going for a walk."

"Where to?" he says. And he wonders, What happened particularly the last time I met her at Kennedy Airport? "Where are you going?" he says, standing there.

"Van Cleef's," she says.

"What for?"

"To buy a present."

"Who for?"

"Myself," Elsa says.

"Oh," says Paul. "Well that's all right. What happened particularly the last time I met you at the airport?"

"It was some years ago."

"Years? What are you talking about? I picked you up at Providence last October. I met you at San Juan, September. Then, July—"

"No, you haven't been to Kennedy to meet me for years. When I've been to Europe these last years somehow it's happened you couldn't meet."

"Well," he says, putting his memory straight as she unpacks her jewellery, piece by piece. "Well, maybe you're right. I can't remember when I last met you at Kennedy."

"It was Idlewild then, 1960."

"It couldn't be so long ago. What happened?"

"You drove me straight to the clinic on Long Island and had me locked up."

"Now look, Elsa," he says.

"You said you were taking me to Poppy Xavier's. Instead I found myself being expedited in the wrong direction."

"Elsa!"

"And we pulled up outside the main door of the clinic and I got hustled in by those blue-robed horrors."

"Oh, shut up, Elsa. We were only trying to help you."

"Who's 'we'?"

"All of us," he says, limply.

"That means you alone. That's what 'all of us' means."

"Well, I tried to help you. Pierre knows that. So does Katerina. What's the point of going over it all again?"

"Only that I'm sure I wouldn't let you meet me with the car at Kennedy Airport again. I flew to Paris and chartered a jet from there. Here I am."

"I was trying to help you. I always try to help you," he shouts.

"You'll be charged with shouting and inveighing. Isn't

that a crime? I'm sure it is. Anyway, the point is, I'd love you not to help me. The point is, I can help myself, thank you."

"You're mad," he says, quietly.

She closes her jewel case, smiling.

He says, "Chartering a jet. You need help."

"Help is a hindrance to me."

The hall porter pushes in the door with two suitcases. He is followed by Garven.

Garven is wearing a bath-robe of pink-striped towelling. His hair, yellow-grey, stands round his head like a lifted halo. He hasn't had time to put in his contact lenses and is wearing a pair of spectacles which make him look different from usual.

Elsa laughs. "Good morning, Garven," she says. "How've you been?"

"Good morning. How have I been? I've been about as usual. I've been waiting for you, it's been a worry. Why did you go away like that, without warning?"

"Is this place getting on your nerves, Garven?" She turns to the porter. "Oh, thank you, thank you. Mr. Hazlett will . . ."

Paul fishes out his note-case and extracts a note, his fingers like pincers.

"Good-bye now, thanks, lady, you're welcome," says the porter as he leaves.

"Garven only wants to help you," Paul says.

"What a lame, lame, statement. I feel I want to help it over a stile," Elsa says.

Paul says to Garven, "She's in that sort of a mood."

"We thought you might be catching a late plane, Elsa," says Garven, feeling his unshaved chin.

"I waited for your call, Elsa," Paul says.

She goes into the drawing-room flanked by her walking shadow and followed by Paul and Garven. "Pretend I'm poor," she says. "Poor and crazy; just of no account."

"Would you like some coffee, Elsa?" Garven says.

"Yes, please," she says.

Garven flaps off in his gown and slippers while Paul sits down, watching her.

He says, "Pierre's play opens tonight. He kept seats for us in case we could make it. I said I'd let him know if you arrived in time."

"We could let him think I haven't arrived yet."

"We should go and see our son's play. It should be a success."

"Whose play? I thought *Peter Pan* was written by J. M. Barrie."

"Yes, but the production is Pierre's idea. All old people. Very original, you must hand him that."

"I'll think about it," she says. "I'll see how I feel when I get back from my shopping."

"You look well."

"Thanks. I'm on a new diet. Over-ripe tomatoes. Very rejuvenating." She presses the service bell, leans back her head and closes her eyes. After a while Garven comes in with a coffee-tray. "Did you ring?" he says.

Elsa opens her eyes. "I want some over-ripe tomatoes for my new diet."

"Over-ripe?—Not merely ripe?"

"Mushy. The bacteria have a rejuvenating effect."

"Those Swiss cures," says Garven, "are . . . um, well . . ."

"She looks all right," says Paul. "My wife looks good."

"Where would I buy rotten tomatoes?" Garven says, looking straight at her shadow.

"Get me the Princess Xavier on the phone," Elsa says. "She has plenty of everything."

Elsa comes into the drawing-room. Paul gasps. She is wearing a flame-coloured crepe evening dress with dark beads gleaming at the hem and wrists. She wears a necklace and earrings made of diamonds and rubies. Her fingers are a complex of the same sparkling stones. She is wearing a diamond bracelet. She is saying "good evening" to Paul while he gasps and to Garven while he stares. Paul is wearing casual black trousers, a green velvet coat and a black turtle-neck sweater. Garven wears a brown tweed coat, light fawn trousers and a shirt of blue-and-fawn check, open at the neck, where, inside the collar, a small dark blue silk scarf is knotted.

Paul speaks. "You can't go like that, Elsa," he says. "You'll be lynched. You'll be robbed. Do you realise where the theatre is? It's somewhere off Houston Street away downtown."

"It's the opening night," Elsa says. "My son's play by J. M. Barrie."

"Elsa," says Garven, "this job is too much for me."

"You make more as my butler than you ever did as a doctor," she says. "However, if you want a raise I can give you a raise."

"I don't want even to be your analyst any more," Garven says. "It isn't a question of money, it's a question that you're eating away my life in nibbles. A nibble here and a nibble there. Sometimes I wake in the morning and wonder if I'm still alive."

"Now you know what it's like," Paul says. "I've had a life-time of it."

She looks at herself in the gold-framed oval glass, touches the jewels in each ear and says, "You leave this house with-out a stain on your character. Don't you like my dress? I borrowed the jewels from Van Cleef. They're not fake, though. It's just that it was too much trouble going to the bank, and there wasn't really time to arrange for the detective-escort. I'd like a vodka tonic." She sits down. "Van Cleef usually oblige."

"You look like something from the Garment District. What do you want to carry that big crocodile bag for?"

"It's Poppy's bag. I promised to return it. I borrowed it months ago to carry some shoes in that I wanted copied at the shoemaker."

The front door rings.

"There's Poppy, it must be her. Garven, open the door for the Princess, and I would like a drink."

The bell rings again, louder, and Garven, shaking himself out of his state of near-hypnosis, jerks his gaze away from Elsa, turns and goes to open the door.

"Elsa," says Paul. "This is a very small theatre in a very back street. It's not only off-Broadway, it's very off off-Broadway. Experimental. Don't you understand?"

In sails the Princess Xavier, shedding her sable wraps, to reveal herself in many folds of fair lace and flesh. She, too, is bearing a selection of jewels about her person, and al-though they are less new and floodlit than Elsa's, some of the diamonds being of the old cut which blacken through time, still, the total effect evidently does not strike Paul and Garven as being suitable. Paul stands perfectly still. Garven disappears with a frightened glance and can be heard treading softly towards the kitchen as if he can not believe the sound of his footsteps in his own ears. He can then be heard emptying ice from the tray into the ice bucket.

Meanwhile, the embraces between the Princess and Elsa, fraught with wafts of lace and spangles like a little Dance of the Seven Veils, are taking place. "It must be a proud evening for you, Elsa," says the Princess as she gathers her robes about her, finally, on the sofa.

"I came back by jet, I chartered a jet, specially to make it," Elsa says, sitting beside her on the sofa, erect, with her body turned towards the reclining Princess and half of her behind overlapping the sofa's edge. Elsa at the same time droops her eyelids, inclines her head romantically and sighs. Then she turns round and makes herself comfortable, pounding the cushions into place behind her.

"You know, Poppy," she says, "I've been thinking. My psyche is like a skyscraper, stretching up and up, practically all glass and steel so that one can look out over everything, and one never bends."

Paul sits down opposite them. "Garven would be sorry to miss that bit," he says. Garven can be heard returning. He comes in with a tray and a bucket of ice-cubes.

"Are you feeling better?" says the Princess to Garven. Paul jumps up and busies himself with the drinks, while Garven, putting down the tray, hesitates what to reply.

"You look all right, really," says the Princess.

"I haven't been sick," Garven says.

"That's the attitude I like to hear," the Princess says. "One should always conceal one's problems."

"What problems?" Garven says.

"Poppy, what will you drink?" says Paul, while Elsa

laughs a little, then stops. "Poppy," Elsa says, "you are skating on thin ice."

"For you, also, vodka?" Paul says to the Princess. His heart's panic begins to rotate; I'm on the wrong train, he silently screams, an express train going miles in the opposite direction from where I want to go, and I can't get off.

"You're all mad," says Garven, looking defiantly at Paul as if lacking the courage to direct himself at Elsa.

"A rye on the rocks for me," says the Princess. "I left your rotten tomatoes on the hall table. How do you eat them? Do they go through the blender?"

"There's a special process," Elsa says.

"Well, I'm quitting," Garven says. "So you needn't explain your special process to me."

"The last time I came here," says the Princess, "Garven gave in his notice. I clearly remember."

"No, that was the maid. She never came back," says Elsa.

"Oh, Garven or the maid, one of them," says the Princess. "You can't count on anyone these days, can you?" She has taken her drink from Paul, who now gives Elsa her vodka and tonic. He looks at his watch.

"We've got time," says Elsa.

"It starts at seven-thirty," Paul says. "Hadn't you better go and change?"

"Certainly not," Elsa says. "Imagine," she says to the Princess. "It's my son's opening night and he wants me to go dressed like a hippie. He should be wearing a dark suit, at least."

"I always dress," says the Princess. "Always have done and always will."

Suddenly Garven moves towards them, then stops. He

opens his mouth wide, then says in a high-pitched top note, "Sick!" He then shuts his mouth tight and turns to pour himself out a trembling drink.

"Garven," says the Princess as they stand waiting for Elsa to get her coat, "I can get you a remarkable job with a very delightful couple who have a triplex at Sixty-eighth and Park. Everything they have is an *object d'art*, including the teaspoons."

"Thanks, I'm going back to my practice," Garven says, and sighs.

"He's a professional man," says Paul.

"I've wasted time," says Garven. "If she wants my services in future, she'll have to come to my office."

Paul takes out his handkerchief and pats his forehead here and there. "This apartment kills me," he says. "It's antiquated. The heat's terrible. You can't control it. Poppy, can't we talk to Elsa about moving to a new apartment? I've tried for years. She won't listen to me."

"One gets attached to one's home," Poppy says. "Can't you have it fixed? Open the window."

"It's open," says Paul. "But the heat wins."

Garven says, "I'd have all the air conditioners turned on full if I had my way."

"She likes the heat in winter," says Paul.

"It's good for the palm tree," says the Princess, looking at the flourishing plants in the corner.

"I tell you what, Poppy," says Paul. "She has too much money. Some women can't take it. In the old days when she didn't have so much she was more amenable to reason."

"Ha, ha, so was I," says the Princess. "But I'm healthier and happier now, and so is Elsa."

"I agree with Paul," says Garven. "Not on every point, but on this one."

Elsa calls out from the hall, "Come on, I'm ready."

Princess Xavier is carefully handled out of her hollow on the sofa by Paul and Garven and is escorted to the hall where Elsa is waiting.

"You can't go like that," Paul says.

Elsa is wearing a long coat of white fox fur.

"I bought it in Paris," she says, "for this occasion."

"I believe in style," says Princess Xavier, who, with the help of Garven, is being enfolded in her voluminous sable coverings, which give off little wafts of something that smells like a strange incense but is in reality a mixture of camphor and a scent named *Diane du Bois*. How long, cries Paul in his heart, will these people, this city, haunt me? "Elsa," he says, "be yourself. Just be yourself, I ask you."

They are driving through the streets in Princess Xavier's Rolls. A long journey through the traffic, with the Princess's chauffeur muttering quietly all the way down Second Avenue. He stops to let them off at a convenient corner, conspicuously. And nervously Paul and Garven propel the women in haste along the narrow pavements. A girl tries to block Elsa's path, saying in a slow solemn voice, "That is too much," but Paul pushes his wife ahead causing the girl to stumble and bump into Garven who follows with the Princess. "Wait a minute," says the girl to Garven, but he waits not at all, barging past the other pedestrians with his charge, the breathless Princess. Paul is watching the street numbers with shifty eyes. He stops at a doorway between a delicatessen shop and a Mexican art gallery. A woman comes to the door of the delicatessen, followed by a young boy. "They robbed their grandmother's tomb," says the woman.

"This must be it," says Paul, pushing Elsa through a

doorway between the two shops where a signboard announces:

VERY MUCH CLUB

ADVANCED THEATRE.

Followed by Garven and the Princess they file along a bright-lit passage to a curtained doorway. Here, tickets are being collected and sold by two lean young men who are accompanied by a group of supporters. One of them is Pierre, who has now grown a small beard and is wearing a white turtle-neck sweater and red velvet trousers. His friend beefy Peregrine, with Katerina leaning on him in a stupefied way, stands by. Peregrine says to Pierre, "Here comes your tribe."

A girl holding a bundle of programmes comes forward to greet them. "Good evening," she says. "I'm Alice." A young man standing beside her says, "I'm Ken."

"Really?" says Elsa. "You don't look it."

Pierre turns as his mother speaks. She is already causing a stir, but Pierre looks at her languidly, as one well accustomed to absorb any shock. Katerina sways a little, stands lankily upright for a moment, then leans back on bulky Peregrine. "Am I on a trip or is she real?" Katerina says.

"Both," says Elsa.

"We'd better get to our seats," Paul says uneasily, taking Princess Xavier's arm to edge her out of the little crowd. Garven follows with an anxious, trapped look.

"Wait a minute," says Elsa, "I want to see these photographs." She pushes through a cluster of people who, now somewhat hypnotised, make way for her.

On a wall a poster announces the show *Peter Pan* – UN-EXPURGATED, followed by a list of the cast. This is flanked by numerous large stills of the play. An aged baby-faced Peter Pan with his elfin cap holds up to his old lips with knobby fingers a grandiose horn. The caption reads, "Miles Bunting, the Broadway veteran, plays Peter, the boy who never grew up."

"Well, Poppy," says Elsa to the Princess, "what do you think of this? Miles Bunting. Is it the same Miles Bunting we used to work with during the war? Remember, at the Compound?"

"He was a professor of something," says Princess Xavier, scrutinising the photograph. "He was never an actor." She turns to Paul. "Do you remember Miles Bunting?" she says.

Paul is looking over her shoulder at the photograph. Something has gone wrong, he is thinking. Life can't be like this, I simply don't accept it. He says, "To me, it looks the same man, greatly altered of course. Much fuller in the face. But the mouth, the nose, the eyes, all the features in fact. The name alone could be a coincidence, but the face . . ."

"Lady, you come to the wrong playhouse," says a man's voice behind them.

A girl laughs, then Pierre's voice says, "My mother has come to the right place."

"And there's Wendy," says Elsa. Who's playing Wendy? Anyone we know or used to know?"

"Curly Curtiss," the Princess reads in a loud voice from the caption. The picture is that of a haggard and bony woman with glittering eyes and wild long white hair. "I don't recall any Curly Curtiss, though, do you, Paul?"

Paul does not reply.

"What's curly about her?" Elsa says, peering at the picture.

Garven says, "I think we ought to move on. I really think we should take our seats as unobtrusively as possible."

At which Katerina comes out of her trance and gives a loud unearthly laugh.

They troop into the little theatre, through the curtains held open impassively by Pierre. He follows them, guiding them with his voice, "Right down to the front. There are four seats reserved in the front row."

The theatre is already almost full. Someone in the audience has started to applaud as Elsa and the Princess appear. Then a few others applaud merrily. "She left her tiara in the bank," says someone.

"Leave her alone," yells another voice. "She's free to wear what she likes isn't she? Like you're free and I'm free."

Elsa, settling in her seat, lets her white foxes fall from her shoulder.

"Those jewels real?" says someone.

Princess Xavier, who has been settled with difficulty in her seat between Garven and Paul, now makes further difficulties for them by rising. She turns to the audience and calls out, "Our jewels are as real as you are."

This wins further applause.

The Princess allows herself to be helped back into her seat, complaining, "We've been far-out longer than they have."

A man slinks down the aisle, and takes a flash picture of the group of four. Paul starts with fright. Garven looks fiercely at Elsa. But the house has filled and the hubbub becomes a murmur. Soon a hush falls and the curtain rises.

"It's a crime to do this to a little kids' entertainment," someone says after the first act. "It's sick."

"Sick is interesting. Sick is real."

All the same, laughter has arisen, has roared and has filtered away to silence again and again during the first act.

"I find it a bit baleful," says the Princess.

"It's a great idea," says Garven. "It gives you another dimension, seeing all those old hands. Peter Pan was really good when he flew in. It must have been a strain on the old fellow. I must say it was hilarious. It's going down well. It's—"

"Garven's enthusiasm," says Elsa, "tells me a lot about Garven. I wonder what the people who licensed the play are going to do when they find out that it's being presented as an obscene show."

"It isn't obscene," says Garven. "That's to say, Peter Pan's a deeply relevant psychological problem."

"There's going to be trouble," Elsa says.

"What can they do?" says Paul. "They've licensed the play. I went into this angle with Pierre when I put up the money. The trustees don't have any casting rights. All the novelty of the interpretation is in the cast. Nothing else is changed. Old people instead of young."

"Well, we haven't seen it all yet," says the Princess.

"It can't go wrong," Garven says emphatically to Elsa. "I'm wild about it. I'm . . ." He stops as he sees her shadow moving beside her as she turns to adjust more comfortably her voluminous white furs. Paul, noticing Garven's sudden silence, looks towards Elsa, too. He sees that she has on her lap the large crocodile leather bag. "I thought you said that bag was Poppy's," he says.

"So it is."

"Well, it's unsuitable. Vulgar. But anyway, you just

don't look at all right, so what does the handbag matter? It's been embarrassing for Garven and me. Let alone Pierre."

The lights dim—Elsa settles back in her seat among the white fox furs and Garven once more shifts his mesmerised stare to watch the curtain rising.

The scene is the traditional Never-Never Land, the island of Lost Boys. Garven breathes heavily with psychological excitement as Lost Boys of advanced age prance in fugitive capers with the provocative pirates, then hover over the crone, Wendy. Enter, Peter Pan. At this point Elsa stands up and starts throwing squelchy tomatoes one after the other at the actors. One soft tomato after the other she brings out of the big crocodile bag. The tomatoes land fairly accurately. Her principal aim seems to be Peter Pan played by Miles Bunting, on whose head Elsa lands two large tomatoes, and on whose retreating back she lands one.

The curtain is urgently brought down and meantime a certain pandemonium has broken out. A man behind Elsa climbs over the seat and pulls at her hair. A woman clutches Elsa's jewelled necklace. Garven is trying to drag the Princess away from the scene while Paul is doing his best to explain to Elsa's attacker that his wife is of delicate temperament.

Suddenly out of nowhere, as if wafted through the air like Peter Pan and Tinkerbell themselves, the police are on the spot. The people at the back begin to leave the theatre, but those at the front are caught up in a general riot in which many members of the audience, assuming that some group of justified political contesters is responsible for the tomato throwing, hurl insults at the police. Three policemen fight their way to the front where Elsa is on the

floor being shouted at by the man who had come from behind her.

Elsa looks up at the officers of the law. "I'm the mother
of the author," she says, and is duly rescued, bearing the
Princess with her. Paul follows humbly, explaining that he
is the father. Numerous hippies and Negroes and bearded
scholars, various tax-paying residents of Greenwich Village and other members of the audience, including Garven,
who are trapped in the front two rows, are arrested and
taken away by the police in a large van.

Outside the theatre, Paul is saying wildly to a police
officer, "Those people are not real. My son, my wife, my
daughter, do not exist."

"No?" says the policeman.

Elsa is meanwhile sitting with the Princess on a sofa in a
little room off the foyer, awaiting the arrival of safe trans-
portation. Elsa checks her jewellery and finds all pieces
intact, as also does the Princess.

"Such a wild crowd," says the Princess. "These days one
isn't safe anywhere. One can't even go to the theatre in
peace."

"I quite agree," says Elsa.

Chapter Six

"Go back, go back to the grave," says Paul, "from where I called you."

"It's too late," Elsa says. "It was you with your terrible and jealous dreams who set the whole edifice soaring."

"You're not real. Pierre and Katerina don't exist."

"Don't we?" she says. "Well then that settles the argument. Just carry on as if nothing has happened all these years."

He puts down the newspaper he had been holding. He says, "The headline reads, 'Offbeat Production *Peter Pan* Ends in Tomato Throwing.' You've ruined Pierre's show. Your own son's show."

"If Pierre doesn't exist and I'm dead," she says, "I don't see how I could have ruined his show. Use your logic."

"Read the paper yourself. See the headlines. You know it was you who threw the tomatoes."

"I know," she says, "and I stopped the show. Tell Garven to bring some more coffee." She hands him the coffee-pot from the breakfast tray. He takes it and stands staring at her, adjusting the tie-belt of his dressing-gown. She says, "But I wasn't to blame for the big blackout in 1965. You were so sure it was me. But then you saw in the papers that it was someone who forgot to shove in a plug or put on a switch or something when he went off duty. So you see, you can be wrong about me, Paul. You can make mistakes. You can be mistaken about anything."

He goes to the kitchen with the coffee-pot and can be heard speaking to Garven. Their voices can be heard, conversing there. The words are undiscernible but the sounds are of an unusual accord. It is like the conversation of men who have shared a house for years and are used to each other's ways; the tones of voice do not reach very high or low registers; there is here and there a little force behind a phrase, as of indignation or resentment, quickly followed by an equal, altogether acquiescent response. The voices lower, as in confidential exchanges. It is like the distant sea. The voices trail away as in reciprocal exasperation. Elsa, in the drawing-room, trails her shadow in the morning light, to the telephone table. She sits beside it, staring reflectively, and when Garven and Paul arrive with the coffee, wearing on their faces identical expressions, they find her in that position.

Garven carries a tray on which are a plate of curly buns, a dish of butter, a dish of marmalade, three breakfast plates and an extra cup and saucer. Paul carries the percolator.

"I'm going to have my breakfast here with you," Garven says. "We have to talk."

"Would you mind fetching a duster?" Elsa says. "The phone's dirty. Black marks round all the numbers. You have to remember to dust in between the crack with the edge of the cloth. It looks awful."

Paul puts out one hand reassuringly towards Garven and with the other hand removes his clean white handkerchief from his pocket and gives it to Elsa. "Clean it with this," he says.

She slides the edge of the handkerchief into the dusty crevices of the dialling disc and slides it round the surface of the numbers. "It must seem funny to you," she says, not speaking specially to either of them, "to see this deadly body of mine in full health, dusting the dust away."

Paul takes the tray and moves it to a table farther away from her as if she might continue, so spoiling his breakfast. Garven joins him.

"I'd like some coffee, now," Elsa says, casting aside the handkerchief. She starts to dial a number. Paul pours her coffee and brings it over to her while she speaks into the telephone. "Oh hallo, is Miss Hazlett at home?" she says.

Paul moves back to his breakfast while Elsa puts her hand over the telephone and says to him, "It's a man." She uncovers the speaker and says, "I'm her mother, Countess Janovic-Hazlett. Who are you?"

"Elsa!" says Paul. Elsa looks away from the phone and says without covering it, "She's got a man there, at this hour of the morning. He's the one called Merlin. Do you remember Merlin, the boy she brought home in the summer?" She directs her mouth once more to the receiver and says, "I didn't recognise your voice, Merlin. I thought it was Gene or Harry. They've been currently staying to breakfast with Katerina. Tell her I called." She clicks the receiver-rest with her finger then starts to dial another number.

Garven says, "I'm going to reconstitute my Institute of Guidance. I'm going back to pick up where I left off." He butters his roll and Paul butters his. They eat, they sip their coffee, in unison.

"Hallo," says Elsa, "This is the Countess Janovic-Hazlett calling. I want to talk to Mr. Mueller alias Kiel."

"Elsa!" says Paul.

"Mr. Mueller," Elsa repeats. Then after receiving the reply, she says, "Why isn't he in? It's after nine-thirty and the store opens at nine. Have him call me. Countess Janovic-Hazlett. It doesn't matter how you spell it; he'll know who it is." She puts down the receiver.

"What's the matter?" she says. "Why do you keep interrupting me?"

"You mustn't call yourself Countess like that."

"Well, it's your title."

"Do you have a title?" says Garven to Paul.

"My father was an Englishman," Paul says.

Elsa says, "This particular title is inherited from his mother. By special dispensation of Elizabeth of Hungary."

"Well, I gave it up," Paul says. "At least, I never even took it on."

"His mother called herself Countess."

"In Montenegro," says Paul, "you are noble if you own two goats on a mountainside. My mother didn't even have that. Only debts."

"Well, I'm calling myself Countess," says Elsa.

"This is America," Paul says.

"Let her call herself Countess," Garven says. "If it makes her feel good why shouldn't she call herself Countess?"

"It's outrageous," Paul says, "starting all that up again now."

"Long live the outrage!" Elsa says. "Long live the holy outrage. I sold Katerina to Mueller for fifteen hundred dollars one night and cheap at the price."

"She doesn't know what she's saying," says Paul to Garven.

Elsa goes to the window and moves her chair to look out on the East River, taking the telephone with her on the long wire. "Nothing but drizzle and sour soot," she says, looking out.

Paul pours a second coffee for himself and Garven. "More coffee, Elsa?" he says.

"I took Katerina to Mueller's apartment on West Thirty-third," she says. "Katerina was curious about him, she'd heard so much from you, that he was Kiel, Kiel, Kiel. So we went along, and he prepared a dinner in the kitchen. He asked Katerina to help him and while she was there I slipped away. So Katerina stayed on for dinner and stayed all night. I made him give me seven hundred and fifty beforehand and seven hundred and fifty afterwards, he was so keen to sleep with Katerina. She tosses in with everybody, so why not him? Then she said she caught the clap from him. What a lie! I don't get fifteen hundred from everyone she sleeps with." She dials a number.

"Poppy?" she says. "Well, Poppy," she says, "good morning, how are you? . . . Do you know the latest, Paul says I'm not real. He says I died long ago. That means that you're dead too, and Katerina and Pierre were never born. It means that Garven isn't real, either, else how could he have been my Guidance Director for a year and a half and my butler for all these months? Just think of Pierre's friends and Katerina's friends, just think of Paul's awful little analyst, Annie Armitage, and his colleagues; and my money isn't real either. What did you think of the review of Pierre's play?—The review in this morning's paper isn't real and the play wasn't real, of course, but—"

Paul has grabbed the telephone from her and speaks into it to Princess Xavier. "Poppy," he says, "Elsa isn't herself this morning, that's all. . . . No, I don't think she should talk any more, Poppy. . . . No, I don't think I should put her back on, really, Poppy. . . . Well, Poppy, it's up to you. . . . Yes, of course, darling, you're real. Here's Elsa." He hands Elsa the phone.

She looks out of the window at the East River and continues, "I think they want me back in the nut-house, Poppy. . . . Yes, you're quite right. . . . Well, you know what I thought of the play, I demonstrated, didn't I? I have a right to demonstrate as much as anyone else. All right, Poppy. . . . All right, yes, we'll talk later. 'Bye."

She puts down the telephone and says, "Poppy thinks you should go to the nut-house, not me."

"I didn't say anything about nut-house," Paul says.

"I was talking to Garven."

"I'm quitting," Garven says, gathering up the breakfast tray. "Getting booked into the police office for you is asking too much. Last night was too much."

Paul follows him into the kitchen and again the men's voices can be heard. They are discussing. Elsa starts singing to herself, as if unable to explain the reason for her sadness; the voice is small, the notes true. Her shadow spreads from her chair across the carpet in the weak light and, although at this hour of the morning it happens to fall at precisely the correct angle relative to the risen sun, it will certainly continue to fall in this direction all day, wherever she may be.

The telephone rings. It is Katerina. "Oh it's you," says Elsa. "Good morning; I called you. . . . Yes, I know it's Merlin you've got there, he told me. I thought Merlin was Pierre's boy. With a name like that he should be. Your father's in the kitchen discussing me with Garven, they're

like a couple of disgruntled parlour maids this morning.
Yes, I saw the review. . . . What do you mean? . . . Yes,
of course it was me who threw the tomatoes. I didn't like
the play. I knew before I got there I didn't like it. . . .
Well, I'm glad you see my point of view. Garven got taken
to the police station and they released him at two o'clock
in the morning, so I don't see what he's got to gripe about.
I pay him a fortune. He says he's quitting. I wish he would.
. . . No, I haven't heard from Pierre, I expect he's bored
with the whole thing already. Now your father tells me
I'm not real, I died one time and he brought me back from
the grave. . . . Yes, but he's said it before and now he's
starting again. . . . Well, it's only the eighteenth of the
month, what do you do with your money? All right, but
you should make do with your allowance. All these men,
one after the other. Don't any of them have any money? It
isn't the money I mind, it's the principle. . . . You mean
today? No, I can't. I'll call you later and let you know.
You could pick up the cheque; I'll leave it downstairs if I'm
going out. I'll call you later. 'Bye."

Paul comes back, followed by Garven.

Elsa says, "I just spoke to Katerina. Did you hear the
conversation, either of you?"

"No," says Garven.

"No," says Paul. "Why?"

"I just wondered if I was real, that's all. Imaginary people can't very well have telephone calls outside of their
owners' imagination."

"Who said you were imaginary?" Paul says. "I wish you
were imaginary."

"Oh, good. Now we're all real, then?"

He looks at her shadow. "You've become real. That's
the trouble," says Paul.

"Paul's at the end of his tether," Garven says, "and no wonder."

"Why doesn't he go to the clinic for a rest?" Elsa says.

"We were thinking, Elsa, that you might think of taking a cure in a better little clinic, much better, that I know of right here in Manhattan where you can be near everyone, and the children can pop in and see you every day. Paul can pop in. You would be free to come and go as you pleased. At any minute you could just check out if you didn't like it."

"I don't need a rest," Elsa says. "I have a nice comfortable home. What do I need a clinic for?"

"Free," says Garven, "to leave whenever you pleased, and—"

"Except that there would be difficulties if I did. Once in, you would be able to bring your cooked-up evidence to persuade me to stay voluntarily or else be committed to an asylum for the mad. I remember my former analyst, the last time, at that place on Long Island. He kept on saying, 'It's either here or Bellevue, Elsa.' Never again, thanks. Anyway, he died in a car crash. Served him right."

"Elsa!" says Paul. "It was a tragedy. A very fine analyst."

"He never noticed my beautiful shadow."

"Why should he notice it? People don't look at shadows. It was just by chance that Garven—"

"Oh, no, it wasn't by chance," Garven says. "I'm unusually observant, remarkably so, that's all."

"That's what I mean, Garven," says Paul.

Garven says, "Anyone who had that shadow pointed out to them—anyone responsible in the field of parapsychology, for instance, would be inclined to agree that Elsa should be detained for observation."

"I know," says Elsa, "that there's a fortune in my shadow.

But it's speculative. Happily for me I've got money that isn't speculative, it's real. I can buy anyone off, including you."

"It's too hot in here," Paul says. "I'm going to get these radiators fixed so we can live in a more moderate temperature."

The telephone rings. Elsa answers it. "Hallo. Oh, it's you. I rang you at the store but you hadn't come in. Where are you calling from? . . . Really? Why? . . . Well, I've been having a little chat with my husband and my butler. My husband still thinks you're Helmut Kiel, the spy. I must say you look remarkably like the man. Except that it was back in 1944 when we knew him and you would have aged since then, wouldn't you? My husband thinks I had an affair—"

"Elsa!" says Paul.

"My husband is really a count," Elsa continues. "My butler thinks I'm mad and he threatens to leave. What are you doing tonight?"

Paul grabs the phone from her hand and bangs it down on the receiver.

"Garven," says Elsa, "pick up the newspaper from the floor. It looks untidy. The cleaning woman isn't coming today so you'll have to cope by yourself. I'm going out. I have to take the jewellery back to Van Cleef's."

"Back in 1944," Paul says, "you were sweet and rather gentle."

Shadowed by her shadow she walks across the carpet. Soon she can be heard opening and shutting drawers in her dressing-room, and finally, with business-like footsteps, she leaves the apartment by the East River where Garven and Paul remain alone in the stupefying hot air of the winter morning.

"You know," says Garven, watching Paul as he sits with the newspaper in his hand, "you're an interesting man, Paul. You could be a study in yourself."

"What do you mean?" Paul says, looking up. He's starting on me, he tells himself in his panic. Now he's on to me. "Let's continue to concentrate on Elsa," Paul says. "She's our problem. One thing at a time— As we were saying, there in the kitchen, she's her own worst enemy, and the best thing for Elsa would be a totally new environment. She—"

"An interesting man," muses Garven.

She stamps her left foot. "They fit," she says, "but they look so awful."

"You have to have more boots, Elsa," he says. "Everyone wears boots. What can you do?"

"I really don't often do the same as everyone else does, Helmut. The weather's turning warm now, besides."

"Oh, I know. I know."

"I'll have to ask my husband's advice," she says.

"He stopped by yesterday. He came in to say hallo."

"In here to the shop? Paul came here? What for?"

"He tried to date me," says the salesman. "He wouldn't call me Mueller, he kept on calling me Kiel. He tried to date me for the evening but I told him that I wasn't that way."

"Pierre must have inherited the tendency from his father," Elsa says.

"Your husband," says the salesman in his correct accent, "is under the impression that he and I had a sentimental encounter in the year 1944, and he wishes to repeat the affair as an experiment, in order to establish my identity. However, I explained that I was not yet born in 1944."

"You're a liar," Elsa says. "You know, Helmut, that you were with us at the Compound in England in 1944."

"In our condition of life," says Helmut Kiel, "it isn't possible to lie. Do you want me to keep the boots aside while you think them over or do you want me to send them to your home so that you can show them to your husband?"

"Send them," Elsa says. "Scrawl a message on the soles."

He gives a little bow. She laughs.

"Did you make a date with Paul, then?" she says.

"No. But he says he'll try again." He steps over her shadow and opens the door for her.

She is sitting by the window looking out on the East River.

"Garven," says Paul, "is a dangerous man. He's been shadowing me."

"I need a drink," she says. "Go and get some ice."

"I'm in danger from Garven. Why can't you get the ice yourself? Sitting by the bloody window all day while I'm in danger." He pronounces bloody as "blawdy."

"First it was Kiel, now Garven. You're always in danger from somebody."

"Garven has turned against me. At least, he says he's interested in me," Paul says. "When a man like that says he's interested in you, it's dangerous. Sinister."

Elsa starts to laugh as if in company with the Nothing beyond the window, high above the East River.

"He said he was going to leave us, but he didn't. I wondered why. Now I know," she says to the sky.

"Elsa," he says, listening, "there's the key in the door!"

"I know," she says. "What's the matter?"

"Here comes Garven," says Paul.

"Well, go and conspire with him against me in the kitchen. Get some ice. Ask him to join us for a drink. Say you're having trouble with me."

"He's been following me all day." He goes out and his footsteps pat along the passage to the kitchen. From that distance his voice hums monotonously and so does Garven's.

Elsa gets up with her shadow falling blackly towards the west although the sun is setting in the west window. She goes over to the telephone table, lifts the instrument and trails its long cord back to her window seat. She is dialling a number when Garven and Paul come in, Paul holding the ice bucket and Garven a tray of ice.

"Miss Armitage?" she says.

"Elsa!" says Paul.

"Oh, Miss Armitage," says Elsa, "I'm speaking for Count Paul Janovic-Hazlett. This is Countess Janovic-Hazlett. The Count wishes me to say that if you would care to step over to our apartment for a drink we should be happy to see you. . . . Oh, yes, he's here. Hold on. . . ." She hands the receiver to Paul.

"Annie," he says, "this was unforeseen. Yes, of course she means it. . . . No, Annie, we're very civilised these days and there's nothing to hide. I—" Elsa has grabbed the telephone and, while Garven says, "I hope we're not going to have a scene," Elsa is saying, "When you come I'll read you my daughter's poem about you and Paul. Our daughter, Katerina, is very talented, you know. . . . Oh, yes, Miss Armitage, I think we did meet in the shoe store. . . . Oh yes, but that was a misunderstanding. You're my husband's analyst, yes, I know. . . . But we would simply love to see you in a purely social context. It is very short notice, but Paul . . . How lovely. We'll expect you shortly, then." She replaces the receiver.

"Paul, you look awful, you need a drink. She said she would be over momentarily, which is ungrammatical to my mind, unless she means she only intends to stay for one moment, in which case it's less ungrammatical. It's so difficult to follow people's meanings when they learn the words from Webster's. What's the matter with you, Paul?"

"This is unnecessary," says Paul.

"Vodka and lemon for me," says Elsa. "Garven, I'll leave it to you. A nice lot of vodka, Garven."

Paul starts to shout. "Garven," he shouts. "You're supposed to be a professional man. What have you been saying to Elsa about Annie Armitage?"

"I've never heard of her," Garven says. "Far less spoken of her. I shall be very happy to meet your analyst, Paul. I thought we had come to an understanding, Paul, but we seem to have come to a rift." Garven's voice breaks excitedly. "There's no need to raise your voice at me."

"Garven is going to break down, he'll weep," says Elsa.

"What does it matter," says Paul, "seeing that you're not real, any of you."

"My daughter is a little dumb, as you would put it," Elsa is explaining as she pulls the piece of paper from her handbag. She turns her head from the window towards Miss Armitage.

"You said she was smart," Miss Armitage says. "I took note of it."

"I said she was talented. I didn't say she employed her talent," says Elsa. " 'Now,' " she reads, " 'in the crossroads of my life,'

I do no longer love my wife.
I love Miss Armitage instead
And wish to be with her in bed.

—Just a minute, Miss Armitage, don't—"
"I'm not going to listen to this," says Miss Armitage,
clattering her glass on the side table.
"Elsa!" say Garven and Paul.
"Let me finish—just one little foolish verse. 'My wife
has come to middle age;'

Not so Miss Annie Armitage.
From which you rightly do infer
I like to be in bed with her.

—Cute, isn't it?" Elsa folds the piece of paper with a doting
smile.
"She's not real, Annie," says Paul. "Didn't I tell you?
Haven't I been telling you for years? I dreamt her up. I
called her back from the grave. She's dead, and all that goes
with her. Look at her shadow!"
"No, Paul," says Garven, stepping quickly in line with
Elsa to conceal her shadow. "This is unprofessional. As
Elsa's analyst, I protest."
"I don't understand what the fuss is about, Miss Armitage," Elsa says. Miss Armitage is trying to leave, but Paul,
still proclaiming to the room a general state of unreality,
is holding her back.
Elsa says, "Is she a qualified doctor? Should I address
her as Doctor?"
"What have I been telling you, Annie, all these years?"
says Paul. "She's a development of an idea, that's all. She's
not my original conception any more. She took a life of her

own. She's grotesque. When she died she was a sweet English girl, very sweet, let me tell you."

"Sweet is funny," at last breathes Miss Armitage. "Sweet is very funny indeed. She insulted me once before. I should have known better than come over here."

"She gets paid for it," Elsa says absently. "Paul, don't you pay your doctor? Should I maybe have called her Doctor? . . . Maybe—"

"My patients call me Annie," yells Annie. "Plain Annie. That's part of the routine. I have person-to-person relations with all my patients."

"Annie, look at her shadow," Paul is saying. "Garven, step off Elsa's shadow."

Elsa walks.

"The hell with her shadow," says Annie. "Haven't we got enough serious problems in this city? We already have the youth problem, the racist problem, the distribution problem, the political problem, the economic problem, the crime problem, the matrimonial problem, the ecological problem, the divorce problem, the domiciliary problem, the consumer problem, the birth-rate problem, the middle-age problem, the health problem, the sex problem, the incarceration problem, the educational problem, the fiscal problem, the unemployment problem, the physiopsychodynamics problem, the homosexual problem, the traffic problem, the heterosexual problem, the obesity problem, the garbage problem, the gyno-emancipation problem, the rent-controls problem, the identity problem, the bisexual problem, the uxoricidal problem, the superannuation problem, the alcoholics problem, the capital-gains problem, the anthro-egalitarian problem, the trisexual problem, the drug problem, the civic culture and entertainments problem which is something else again, the—"

"Down there, outside the United Nations," Elsa says, "there are three policemen demonstrating in the nude, except for their caps—that's to show they're policemen. What are they demonstrating for?"

Garven looks out. "It looks like she's right," he says. "See that enormous banner, it says JUSTICE FOR US COPS. And there's a crowd of police giving them active support, and they're cordoned off. The people can't cross the road."

The noise of the demonstration wafts up to the flat. "It's the police problem," says Elsa. "You forgot to mention the police problem, Doctor Armitage."

"I included it by implication," says Annie, and returns to craning down at the demonstration.

"No you did not," says Elsa.

"Elsa!" says Paul.

"I see what you mean by her shadow," Annie says, savagely. She looks at everybody's shadow in turn, then at Elsa's. She turns to face Garven. "You're her analyst, sir?" she says.

"Yes, Annie," says Garven, meekly. "It's a pleasure to meet a colleague, Annie."

"Why don't you take me home?" Annie says. "This apartment's overheated, and all this infraparanormalisation is too much. We can discuss our problems at my place."

"Garven has lost his monopoly on my shadow," says Elsa vaguely to the window as Garven takes Annie's arm, edging her towards the door.

"Where is your coat?" says Garven.

"They will have to come to an agreement," Elsa says. "Fifty-fifty on the proceeds of my shadow. I knew this would happen when she saw it in the shoe shop."

Paul is staring down at the police demonstration. "When the police start demonstrating without their clothes on it's the end of everything. Your dreams . . . everything. The Forty-eighth Street Precinct."

"They'll get pneumonia," says Elsa.

"Look, they're putting on their clothes again," Paul says.

"Yes, they're putting on their trousers, look."

"We'll see it on the television tonight," says Paul. "A slightly censored version."

"Yes, look, the cameras are packing up and going off. The men just posed for the shots."

The front door clicks shut behind Garven and Annie.

"Call the steak shop," says Elsa, "and order dinner for eight-thirty delivered to the apartment."

"We'll see it on the news," says Paul. "At least parts of it."

"She missed out the mortality problem," Elsa says.

Chapter Seven

"Scotch," says Paul. He sits somewhat miserably at a table in the dim back-room of the bar from where, nearly indiscernible himself, he can see the group he is watching. "On the rocks?" says the waiter. "On the rocks," says Paul. "New York is a fun city, says the waiter as he swings away with his tray held high at one shoulder, swiping up some empty glasses from another table as he goes.

It is nearly nine-thirty at night. There has been a pause in the music, and now it starts up again. A large grey-haired man, his ochre-coloured face full of planes, ridges and pouching curves, plays the piano; he is an old-timer from New Orleans. A short man with a ginger moustache and a checkered suit plays the trombone, while a fat young man in a white baggy shirt and grey baggy trousers sits beating the drums with expert boredom. This early jazz music, fast and brazen, does not appear to do anything to Paul's blood-stream. He pays the waiter for his drink and lets it lie, his eyes fixed on the four people who are sitting in the bright-lit front part of the establishment close by the bar and the band. Elsa and Princess Xavier together with two men. One is plainly Mueller from the shoe shop. Not Mueller but Kiel, thinks Paul; no matter what they say I'm almost sure of it. The ice in his drink is melting away. He sips and ponders the second man at Elsa's table.

He has a face recently familiar. Where, thinks Paul, have I seen him the last few days? It is a crumpled, oldish face on a tall body. Maybe I saw him a long time ago, I could have known him somewhere else, at some other time in another country in quite different circumstances. Miles Bunting comes suddenly to mind. He played Peter Pan for Pierre the other night at the first and only performance —Miles Bunting from the Compound during the war, when he was a lanky, handsome, Intelligence officer.

Paul sips his drink with its floating wafers of ice, looking over his glass at the group. They have taken control, he thinks. I didn't mean it this way. This bar could go up in flames and put an end to them all; but no, it won't.

How white are the midnight fields beyond the Compound, under the waxing moon! Miles Bunting comes out of a hut. His face is white with black eyebrows marking it like a fur trimming. Inside the half-open door sits Elsa, crying, her hands folded on the typewriter in front of her.

It is early afternoon and Elsa comes along the road towards him with Poppy Xavier. Elsa is wearing a faded blue dress; her brown arms swing and she is holding a basket of blackberries. The Princess Xavier lumps along beside her, wearing the same baggy trousers she has worn for the duration of the war. "Here's Paul," says Elsa.

"What are you going to do with those?" Paul says, pointing to the blackberries.

"Make jam," says Elsa.

"What are you going to use for sugar?" Paul says.

"My next month's ration and another packet of sugar from Poppy's Care parcel. The only thing we need is jars. We haven't got any jam-jars."

He is sitting with Elsa in the office where Colonel Tylden, the Security officer, sits behind his desk, with a filing cabinet for his bodyguard, packed as it is with information which would amaze the people it describes, so true and yet so lonely and isolated are the motionless little facts.

Here in the country the robot-bombs which are already screaming down over London cannot be heard. The Security Headquarters are a small house in the park of a large house. The small house is surrounded by hedges, well-clipped in spite of the shortage of gardeners. No gardener, however, is likely to be seen. The bare wood of the floors and staircase bear the general marks of wartime neglect but they are dusted and swept. Who dusts, who sweeps, no one could know—the cleaning woman is never seen by the light of day. Here, every day is a Puritan Sunday. The Security staff move about sedately, sounding their consonants like teachers of elocution when they speak at all, measuring their treads, taking pains with their infrequent cigarette ash.

Here in the green depths of England, in this spring of 1944, a perfectly innocent person can panic; better a P.O.W. camp in the green depths of Germany together with one's own unit, all in it together. Paul's mind fidgets around with this thought. Better off in the army, getting ready for the Invasion, preparing, who knows, to meet your death; it is not so very appalling when you rattle and bash over the countryside in an armoured car, in a convoy, and life suddenly comes to an end. Better than burrowing like a mole with secret work under the omniscient eyes of these creeping Jesuses in soldier's uniforms or clean brown corduroys. Colonel Tylden, the Chief of Security comes in. He shakes their hands. He apologises. He pulls up his chair and sits down. Overture to Act I.

Since Paul was last called in, Elsa too has been interrogated alone. After a month's silence, it is still apparently the question of Kiel. Now they have suddenly been invited together. It is almost like a marriage ceremony, so closely does this experience unite them, seeing that the Security officer does not care a damn whether his questions will separate them or not. All he wants to know about is Kiel. What does it matter, Paul thinks, as he feels Elsa's apprehension from where she sits at the opposite angle of Colonel Tylden's desk, half-facing both men—what does it matter what there was between her and Kiel, and what Kiel might have been to me? All that matters is that we've been brought together, at short notice, without chance of rehearsal. It's something, Paul thinks, to know suddenly how much trust there is between us. After all, this experience is something.

"There are just one or two loose ends. . . ." Colonel Tylden pulls at the right-hand drawer of his desk. It does not move. He gives a self-deprecating little laugh. "Locked, I always forget." He reaches to the table behind him, from which he takes a small dark-green government-issue metal box. This he sets before him with due system. He opens the mysterious object. It is nothing but a card-index. Putting his fingers behind the last card at the back he brings forth a key. With this key he opens the locked drawer in his desk, saying with a smile, "Now you know where we keep our secret of secrets." He opens the drawer, pulls out a file, lays it before him, jerks his arms to ease the sleeves of his coat, gets down to business and opens the file.

He thinks we are schoolchildren, Paul thinks, because he himself has the brain of a schoolboy. Colonel Tylden was responsible for taking Kiel on, and plainly he is now trying to make up a report from a lot of tangled irrelevancies in order to distract attention from the fact that he was taken in by Kiel.

"You both saw him frequently, alone," the officer says. "Did you often see him together?"

"Yes, fairly often," Paul says, "and in company with others of course."

"We did have to work with him," Elsa says.

"Oh yes, I know. And you two have been on separate shifts. Did you ever see him together outside working hours? Not separately, but together?"

"We met him in the village not long before he left," says Elsa, "I think."

"We met him about ten days before. . . . Let me think, yes, over a week before he went. We met him in the village about three in the afternoon and stopped to talk about five minutes, that's all."

"What did you talk about?"

"Really, I don't remember," Paul says. "Do you, Elsa?"

"No, it was just a chat, quite cheerful."

"Nothing important, anyway," says Paul, "or we would have remembered." And indeed he is trying to remember what they talked about when he had walked down the village street with Elsa that day, and encountered Kiel.

"Kiel was unaccompanied?"

"Yes, he must have got leave to go out by himself."

"He was in a happy mood?"

"Quite cheerful" Elsa has said, and it is simply true. Colonel Tylden, not by any perceptible movement or expression, but merely by keeping silent three seconds longer than they expect after Elsa has given this reply, appears to think it not true. He goes on. "Cheerful?" he says.

"Yes," says Paul. "I remember at least it was a fine day and I don't see there was anything special for one to be uncheerful about." Colonel Tylden is making a little note on a pad in some tiny cypher. Paul does not let his eyes dwell on this and Elsa also looks politely away from the note-pad. Obviously he is making a memo to check whether the weather was fine in the afternoon ten days before Kiel left or whether it rained.

"It's difficult to be sure of the date," Paul says.

The colonel leans back and folds his arms. "Fine-looking chap, Kiel, don't you think?" He is addressing Paul.

"Awfully good-looking," Paul says. "He could be an advertisement for breakfast food."

The colonel gives a relaxed laugh. He looks at Elsa. "What do you think of him?"

"I thought he was fun," Elsa says, "for a German."

"In what way, fun?"

"His sense of humour," she says. "And one wouldn't have thought he took anything seriously."

"Evidently he did," says Tylden and flicks the papers in the files. What about those loose ends he has to tie up? thinks Paul. When is he coming to the loose ends?

But evidently Colonel Tylden's loose ends are destined to float in the vague cosmos; he discerns that the couple are not to be embarrassed by his questions. He looks suddenly worn out by the problem. He flicks the pages of the file and sighs. After all, he has to take responsibility for Kiel. Half-heartedly he checks various points from the statements he has previously obtained separately from them.

To Elsa: "You went for walks with him. Did you notice anything strange?"

"No," says Elsa. "He once climbed a walnut tree at one o'clock in the morning in between one broadcast and another, but I thought it was fun, not strange."

"Yes, you told me that."

To Paul: "You had this fight with him, of course?"

"Yes," says Paul, "but as I said it wasn't anything to do with the work. It was just one of those things that happen when one is cooped up in a group."

"Quite," says Tylden. And he gives up the struggle, says good-bye, and they leave.

They have put on their shabby raincoats and are walking with their bicycles down the park that leads from Security Headquarters to the main drive. Although they are in the open air, with no one near them, the instinct to keep silent lingers until they have passed through the country gate.

In the broad drive they do not mount their bicycles. It is an avenue of plane trees, dripping with luminous rain. They walk slowly. It would have been possible, Paul thinks, for us to talk sincerely about Kiel if this meeting had not taken place. Now it's too delicate a subject. I will probably never know exactly what Kiel was to her, she will always wonder if Kiel was anything to me. After all this questioning, one's denials and protestations would be slavish. Kiel has talked; God knows what he's said about us.

Innocently Elsa says, "You'd think he had some reason to set us against each other, asking us along together to probe about Kiel."

"I don't think he thought of our feelings," Paul says.

"Tylden just wanted information and if his questions were inconvenient for us, he simply wouldn't care. I see his point of view. It's his job to be ruthless."

"Very embarrassing," Elsa says.

Silently Paul cries, Help me! Help me! I don't want to hear, to know, her story one way or another. "Kiel is gone," Paul says. "Forget him."

"Well, everyone's curious to know what's happened to him."

"I expect news will filter through sooner or later."

They come to the gate of the park, mount their bicycles and ride towards the Compound through the warm rain. "I'll tell you something," Paul says. "Spy or no spy, Kiel is a rotter."

"He's probably a loyal German at heart," she says. "He probably feels justified."

"German or Zulu," Paul says, "if he ever did any good it was by oversight."

The rain has petered out. They dismount at the bridge and stand for a while watching the pebbly river. Since Kiel's departure, Paul has changed his hours of duty to coincide with Elsa's. Four in the afternoon till midnight. Now that Kiel has gone, who knows who else? He thinks of the other men at the Compound, the English, the refugees and the German prisoners. Perhaps, he thinks, none of them can quite replace Kiel for a woman, only, perhaps, Miles Bunting, and Elsa doesn't get on with him. Perhaps none of them, but who knows?

"Don't worry, Paul," Elsa says, suddenly. "Nobody will believe a word Kiel says. How could they?"

"Forget Kiel, he's nothing but a spent breath to us."

He is sitting at his obscure table in the bar on West Fifty-fifth Street. "Same again," he says to the waiter.

"What was it?"

"Scotch on the rocks," he says. He pushes farther away from him a plate of small gherkins that the waiter has put on the table. The band is resting. The bar is now half-full, and more people arrive from time to time through the double doors, pausing to look round for the best vacant spot or perhaps someone they know. Paul tries to focus his hearing amongst the general chatter and laughter, and echoing glass, on the sounds coming from the central table where Elsa is sitting with the Princess Xavier, Miles Bunting and the man who might be Mueller, might be Kiel. The Princess is sitting with her back to Paul, expansively conversing to left and right, with her fur wraps hanging over the back of her chair. Paul watches the lips of the other three, he strains to listen, but catches nothing of what they are saying.

The bar-waiter stops at their table and takes an order: their second round. Elsa nibbles an almond, and laughs. She is looking straight at Paul, now, but does not appear to see him. She is wearing her new red dress with a matching short coat, and over the back of her chair her sable coat, too, is thrown back, the furs, mysterious and rich, spilling over the brown satin lining. Where did she get her money? Where? And what is she doing here in this place at this time? One should live first, then die, not die then live; everything to its own time.

Miles Bunting pays for the drinks when they arrive. He drinks beer; Kiel has a dark Scotch or bourbon placed in front of him with a soda-bottle fizzing from its mouth; Elsa's drink is colourless, vodka or gin as usual, and comes accompanied by a small yellow-labelled tonic bottle. The Princess has ordered something reddish-brown, God knows what it is. The waiter wipes some spilt liquor from the table, flicks the cloth over his other arm and goes to his next customers.

Miles Bunting raises his beer mug towards Elsa with a smile that reveals for a moment through his middle-aged flesh the angular and nervous features of his youth. But why is he toasting Elsa? He was always against Elsa, she was afraid of him. He used to snub her. Paul sees her again as she sat in the prefabricated hut, crying over her typewriter, and Miles Bunting coming out of the door into the moonlight of the Compound. In that past there was no word of the future. How has it come about? Paul thinks, They will have to go back to the dead, they must all go back. The Dixieland music starts up with a shock of sound. The drummer beats the drum and the cymbals, the piano-keys pelt into the bloodstream, the people in the bar either stop talking or start shouting to each other. Elsa leans her elbow on the table, rests her head in her hand and looks dreamily from one to the other of her companions.

Some new arrivals appear at the door, stand awhile looking round and, finding insufficient space, go out again. As they leave, a man in a raincoat with a sheepskin collar makes his way in. He smiles when he sees Elsa's table, makes straight for it and, still smiling, obtains a chair to join the party. He does not speak for a while, indicating as an excuse the music-vibrant air around them.

A young couple come and sit at Paul's table. He shifts his chair politely to make more space for the woman, then scrutinises the couple rather anxiously, timid with some unnecessary fear. Have I seen them before? Do they, too, belong to my life? Paul pulls his glass towards him. The couple are not known to him at all. He looks again over to Elsa's table. It is the man in the raincoat who has just come in whom Paul recognises; he knew who it was, really, the moment he came in. Colonel Tylden. Tylden is here in this bar in the heart of Manhattan, now seated beside Elsa, talking cheerfully to her as if he saw her last week, and the week before that.

The music stops. Paul gets up and goes over to Elsa's table. She is saying. "My son is an aesthete and my daughter is, well, she's still deciding."

Miles Bunting looks up at Paul. "Oh, look who's here!" he says.

"Paul," says the Princess. "Paul," says Elsa. "Make room for Paul," says Princess Xavier, "and get another chair."

"Come away," Paul says to his wife. "Come away, love, they're all dead." He squeezes past the next table to reach for Elsa's sable coat. He presses it round her shoulders and pulls her arm, lifting her to her feet. "Being dead's a drug," he says, "you'll get hooked on it."

"You always said you were coming to America after the war," Colonel Tylden says. "And so you did. I never thought you would."

Elsa wriggles into her coat, laughing lightly.

"Are you going, Elsa?" the Princess says. "Can I give you a lift? My car will be here at ten-thirty. Where are you going? The streets are dangerous."

Elsa's hand is in Paul's and he is drawing her towards the door, where he stops to collect his coat. While he puts it on she stands patiently waiting, smiling in a very amused way towards the table she has left. Paul takes her arm and they go out into West Fifty-fifth Street.

"If we walk over to Fifth we'll get a cab," Paul says.

At the corner of Sixth Avenue they stop at the traffic lights. "Do you know I think those characters are following," Elsa says without looking round.

Paul glances behind. The group are standing at the kerb outside the bar. Princess Xavier's Rolls passes at this moment, and as Paul watches, the driver pulls up outside the bar and gets out. The Princess is helped and eased into the back seat with her wraps. The three men pile in without looking in Paul's direction; the driver returns to his seat and drives west with the one-way traffic towards Seventh Avenue.

Paul turns again to Elsa and takes her arm. "I doubt if they're following us. They didn't look. They've gone," he says. But he stops again to see if, at Seventh Avenue, the car turns the corner, which it does.

He takes Elsa's arm. "It could be that they'll turn the block to meet us," Paul says. The lights at Sixth Avenue have changed and they cross quickly, his hand on Elsa's arm and her feet skipping light-heartedly. When they reach the opposite pavement she says, "Oh, they'll follow us, all right," but she doesn't look back.

Still holding her arm Paul stops at a bright-lit doorway. "We can go in here for a while. It looks like some kind of a nightspot," he says.

The nightspot goes by the name of The Personality Cult, announced in mauve and green lights. Through the door a blue-carpeted staircase descends below street-level to a man in evening clothes who takes the money.

Mirrored walls reflect them in a dim rosy light. They are passed to the coat-check counter and then to an usher who opens a pink-lit shiny door. Paul propels Elsa through the doorway after the man. They come upon a sunburst of colour, sound and movement. Paul stops to blink for a moment while Elsa, ahead, turns back to beckon him on. When he catches up with her she says, "This deadly body of mine can dance, too."

"All right, all right," Paul says. "We'll dance."

Chapter Eight

"After the war," Paul is saying, "Elsa and I are going to settle in America."

It is late in the spring of 1944. Paul, in London with Elsa, has just returned from one of those missions to the United States which only key-people of the British services are sent on. Paul's official place on these trips is a minor one but he is known as an expert on Serbo-Croat affairs and is always called in as an aide when the Balkan situation is to be discussed. Besides, he once, as a journalist, interviewed Tito, and this has given him a unique place in his branch of Intelligence; moreover, his interpretation of Tito's politics and predictions of his moves have proved surprisingly accurate. Thus, Paul has been on his third much-envied trip to New York and has come back to England on a Sunderland aircraft, in the war-time late spring of 1944.

Paul sits half-reclining on the bed in the London hotel, leaning back on the pillows and drinking whisky that he has brought back from Bermuda, where the plane stopped.

Elsa unpacks a parcel of wonders that Paul has brought over for her. She takes out the presents, all unobtainable in England, or rationed—a box of Du Pont stockings, a box of Lanvin soap, a bottle of Chanel No. 5 scent, a white frilly blouse, a purple-brown transparent scarf, a large tin of Ceylon tea, two packets of California raisins and a little antique box to hold saccharine pills. One by one they are looked at and smiled over and gasped about.

Elsa puts them into Paul's suitcase. They are leaving for the country in two hours' time, on the evening train.

She packs her treasures away. Two raps on the door. "Come in," says Elsa without looking up. The door opens a little way, and Colonel Tylden's head, with a jovial off-duty grin, peers round it. Elsa looks up.

"You're back," he says to Paul, looking at the whisky bottle.

"If you bring along your tooth glass," Paul says, "you can have some."

Tylden goes to collect his glass and reappears in the room. Elsa has finished packing, but her bag is still open. The new presents lie on the top. Tylden pours whisky in his glass then pours in some water from the tap of the wash basin. He, like others from the Compound, generally stays at this hotel when up in London on official business. Today there are some more Compound people in the hotel, getting ready to go back to the country. There has been a conference with other Intelligence units. Always, when this happens, the Compound people for a brief time form a friendly sort of alliance which disappears when they are back in the country, hemmed in with their German collaborators.

"How was it?" says Tylden.

"After the war," Paul is saying, "Elsa and I are going to settle in America."

"Good idea," says Tylden, sitting down in a squeaky cane armchair. "Wish I were younger."

Two raps on the door. "They've smelt the booze," Tylden says. Elsa opens the door and in flounces Poppy Xavier in her bulging tweed coat and trousers. A voice in the corridor and then another, laughing.

"There are no glasses," Elsa says. "You have to bring your own."

Poppy Xavier now occupies the cane chair, which seems to feel the strain. Colonel Tylden stands leaning against the wall, his drink in his hand. In the corridor, the sound of retreating footsteps, laughing voices, and the footsteps again, first outside the door and, now, all coming in to the room. Lanky Miles Bunting, holding two glasses, is followed by a man and a woman in British naval officer's uniform. Cheerfully, Paul shares out his bottle. From nearly a mile away comes the muffled thud of a bomb. This is one of the V-2s, for which there can be no warning siren, silently approaching and suddenly landing to demolish.

"Another one of those," says the naval officer.

Poppy says, "In a way I prefer no warning. You don't have to scuttle to the cellar."

"If it's a direct hit," says Tylden, "nothing can save you." As he speaks a second explosion gives out from a distant part of London.

"Tilbury end, I think," says Miles Bunting.

They are settled in their compartment and the train is about to leave St. Pancras station. Poppy Xavier smiles in the window seat. Elsa lolls next to her. Paul is giving a final push to his suitcase, which stands outside in the corridor. Miles Bunting is reading an art book. Colonel Tylden in the seat looking out on the corridor says to Paul, "You've got a good job waiting for you in America, have you?"

"Quite good. Columbia University."

"Good for you."

"And I think we've got somewhere to stay. A rather nice flat belonging to some friends of my family. They'll keep it for us. It looks out on the East River. Do you know New York?"

"I know it well," says Colonel Tylden.

A V-2 bomb hits them direct just as the train starts pulling out. The back section of the train, where they are sitting, and all its occupants, are completely demolished.

"You died, too," says Elsa. "That's one of the things you don't realise, Paul."

"Don't be silly," he says. "I remember standing by the side of the track when they pulled your body out of the wreck. I remember too many things to be dead."

The coloured lights of the nightspot go off and on, at each flicker becoming more subdued until only a dim rose-bathed glow falls on the circular dancing space beside their table. The music has stopped. A waiter brings champagne in a bucket which he pours into two glasses, very skilfully, as if he had eyes that could see in the dark.

"No, Paul," says Elsa. "That was your imagination running away with itself."

Most of the tables are still empty. When the music starts Paul and Elsa dance in the circle of rose-coloured light which presently changes to orange, then to yellow and green, blue and violet, then back to rose-coloured again.

They are alone on the dance floor. They dance together, then apart. A silver-haired man and a much younger woman join them, both incredibly neat like two manicured lady's fingers. The man's hair and thin well-kept face glint green then yellow as do his silver-blonde and smooth partner's. Their shadows follow them across the floor, never touching, bending with the will of the two substances that shed them. But Elsa's shadow crosses Paul's. She dances apart from him, lightly swinging, moving her hips and her feet only a little, but her shadow touches his. The neat shining couple return to their table after a while but Elsa and Paul dance till the music stops.

"Funny I'm not a bit tired, and I haven't danced for ages," Elsa says.

"It was over six years ago," says Paul, "that we last danced together. It was at Katerina's party. How could it all have been a dream?"

"Katerina is a vagary of your mind," Elsa says, "that's all."

"She may have been at one point but she isn't now— Look who's arrived!" says Paul. "Quick, Elsa, pick up your bag." He is draping her coat over her shoulders and tugging her arm. "They've come," he says, peering over to the entrance where four people are being greeted by the head waiter.

Paul hurries the waiter for his check and gives over the money with his eyes still on the new arrivals. Miles Bunting, Poppy Xavier, Colonel Tylden, Helmut Kiel. They do not look as if they are pursuing anybody. Poppy recognises Elsa and with a wave of sleeves starts making her massive way among the dim-lit tables.

Paul is propelling Elsa by a more devious route towards the door. Miles Bunting sees them pass and moves nearer. "Paul!" he says. "Not going, are you?"

Paul does not reply. Elsa says, "Not enough people. The place is dead."

Colonel Tylden, who comes along next, says, "There isn't much night-life anywhere. The slump. Have you seen the Dow-Jones industrial average?"

Paul presses his wife towards the door, collects his coat and precipitates her before him out into the street.

"I don't see what there is to laugh at," Paul tells her, and beckons a taxi to the kerb.

"When a man's angrily in love with you, it has its funny side," she says.

His heart knocks on the sides of the coffin. "Let me out!"

"Stop!" says Paul to the taxi-driver. "We'll get out here," he says.

Elsa says, "There's nothing doing at the St. Regis at this hour. It's past eleven."

"The bar's open, the restaurant's open," he says. He is helping her from the taxi, and he takes his change. "We won't find anyone we know here," he says.

"I'm not dressed for this," Elsa says, when they come to the hotel's late-night restaurant.

Paul is talking to the head waiter. He turns to Elsa. "We have to book," he says. "We didn't book."

The room is full of elegant diners, very much rooted in life, chattering above the music or sedately dancing.

"Shall we wait in the bar?" Paul says.

"I don't know. It looks boring."

"We'll wait in the bar," says Paul to the head man, who does not seem to give any active encouragement to this plan.

Crossing the hotel lobby they see, emerging from the lift, dressed in evening clothes, Garven and Miss Armitage.

"Why this hotel?" Paul says, as if reasoning with himself. "Why are they staying here, of all places? They must be mad."

Garven has seen them, and now so has Miss Armitage. They approach Paul and Elsa with the delighted air of old friends who have not met for a long time.

"How good you look!" says Paul to Annie Armitage.

She looks shyly at Garven.

"Elsa," says Garven, "I'd like to talk to you."

"Come to the bar," says Paul.

But the far is full, and the mural on the wall not to Elsa's taste.

"Let's go downtown," says Elsa. "I want to dance."

"She's having a night out," Paul explains.

They find seats, however, in a public room leading off the lobby.

"I have to tell you," Garven says, "that Annie and I are in love."

"I have to tell you," Paul says, "that the St. Regis Hotel is not the place to be so."

"Here we have separate suites," says Annie.

"We're a professional partnership as well," Garven says. Through Annie I am getting to know you, Paul. It's the secondary associative process of the oblique approach. And through you I have a tertiary oblique approach to Elsa."

Elsa says to Annie, "I think you're low if you're passing on my husband's confidences as a patient after all these years. It's unethical."

"Your opinion doesn't count," Annie replies.

"She didn't get any confidences," Paul says. "She only thought she did."

Garven says, "There are no confidences involved, there's no betrayal at all. Annie is largely what you've made her,

Paul, and by experiencing Annie I can experience you. Then, you see, by the same token, I can experience Elsa."

Annie says, "When we've had enough experience, primary, secondary and tertiary, then we can really start curative treatment on your wife, Paul. I have a new method."

"She doesn't need treatment," Paul says. "She doesn't exist."

"Come now," says Garven, "that's no way to talk."

"Let's get out of here, Paul," says Elsa.

"Mrs. Hazlett," says Annie, "it's only understandable that you should resist treatment. They all resist treatment, all of them. However, my new method, which is already producing first-class results—I can tell you I have clients lining up outside my office and my switchboard's jammed —my new method does not involve the personality of the subject and therefore the impetus to therapy-resistance is obliviated. My new method is strictly biopsychological. I locate in the various organs of the body the psychological disorder and I treat the patient strictly on the basis of the defective organ. Right now I'm treating a patient who suffers from schizophrenia of the pancreas. I have a gentleman with hyperintrospective bladder complicated by euphoria of the liver. I have under my care a manic-depressive kidney, a cardiac superego, a case of hallucinations of the diaphragm and a libidinal spleen. Fixations of the reproductive organs are common. A person can suffer from egomania of the toenails. You name it, I can therapeutise it."

"That reminds me," says Garven, "I have to see my dentist tomorrow morning."

"I have to see my lawyer," Elsa says. "You left me without notice, Garven, and I have no butler. There must be some way that I can sue for damages."

She is pulling her sable coat over her shoulder and Paul's eyes move sadly to the main lobby where some people have just come in.

Garven says, "Here comes that man Kiel. And Princess Xavier with him, and the actor in your son's play—what was his name?"

"Miles Bunting," Paul says, getting up. "He didn't use to look like that. And the other man is Colonel Tylden. Come on, Elsa."

The newcomers are still looking about them and helping Poppy to rearrange her coverings when Paul and Elsa escape them by getting into the lift. They get out with two other people when it stops. They make their way to a noise beyond a folding doorway.

"I think this is where the action is," Elsa says as the doors swing open.

Paul stops her at the threshold. "Elsa," he says, "are we going to have these followers of yours on our heels all night?"

"You started it," she says. "Your suspicions, your imagination . . . Poor Kiel, poor Kiel, and he died in prison."

"Well, you died in a railway train."

"So did you, Paul," she says. "You know you did."

An elderly group of four is coming away from the reception which proceeds beyond the folding doors. Decorously they move round Elsa and Paul who are still arguing on the threshold.

"Was it Tylden, then?" he says. "Could it have been Tylden, after all, who was your lover?"

"Ask him," she says. "Just go down and ask him to rack

his brains and see if he remembers. I expect they're all still waiting around in the lobby."

"Or Miles Bunting? He made you cry. Was it Miles?"

"I need a sandwich," she says, pulling towards the room although he holds her arm. "I need a drink."

"We'll go somewhere for dinner," he says. "Was it Poppy?"

"One will never really know," says Elsa with the air of discussing a distant name. "What does it matter since we all died?"

He lets her proceed through the doorway, following her. A crowd of expensive people are packed into the room where there is a large buffet set at the far end. A waiter approaches with a tray of drinks. Elsa chooses champagne; Paul takes whisky. They are apparently very late arriving, for nobody stands at the door to announce or receive them. But presently a small white-haired man comes up to them and greets them in a jovial voice.

"Come along in, glad you made it. Thank you for your beautiful gift," he says, shaking first Elsa's hand and then Paul's. "Mary!" he calls out, and his tall, bright-eyed wife, her skin wrinkled with a great many years comes slowly through the crowd towards them, making a path with her hands and walking in a very straight line. "See who's here, Mary!" says the old gentleman, looking to his wife for guidance.

"Wonderful!" she says, kissing Elsa. "I haven't seen you in years. Thank you for your beautiful gift. It is really lovely. You know . . . all these people." She looks at Paul, her bright eyes rather tearful.

"We're late, but you know how it is," Elsa says. "We had to come and congratulate you tonight of all nights."

And she says to Paul, looking straight at him, "Isn't it wonderful, Paul, a golden wedding."

"Well, Paul," says the host, "it's been fifty wonderful years with Mary. I can honestly say I've had a wonderful married life."

"Well, this is great. Here's to you both," says Paul. "Mary you look simply fine."

"Alexander has been the perfect husband," says Mary, "and the perfect father."

"Alexander," says Elsa, "you don't look a day older than when we first met you. And neither does Mary."

Alexander beams at Mary.

"Elsa often talks about you. We remember when we first came to America how good you were to us," Paul says.

"Elsa," says Alexander, confident in his progress towards locating the new arrivals in his mind. "Here comes Conrad, our grandson. You remember Conrad?"

Conrad is upon them. "Why, Conrad," says Elsa. "Of course we remember him, but he won't remember us, I'm sure."

Conrad giggles. "Have you had something to eat?" he says.

Paul and Elsa ease across the room to the buffet.

"I'd like some of that lobster salad," Elsa says.

"I imagine he was a business-man," Paul says, looking round the room.

Elsa takes her plate and fork. "We'll see their names in tomorrow's paper," she says.

They say voluble good nights to the golden wedding party and leave in a wash of kisses and tears. Downstairs in the lobby there is no sign of their pursuers. They swing out of the doors and walk up to the Plaza Hotel, where they make for the Oak Room.

"Here we are," says Poppy from a seat near the door. The men stand up and Miles Bunting says, "Paul—Elsa— we've kept a place for you."

But Paul pulls her away and they are out in Fifth Avenue waiting for an oncoming taxi to pull up by the time Miles has followed them into the street.

"What's the matter?" says Miles. "What are you running away for?"

"We've been to a golden wedding and Paul has psycho-neurotic arches; he feels compelled to dance," Elsa explains as Paul bundles her into the back of the cab, gets in beside her and bangs the door shut. "Downtown," says Paul. The taxi purrs on through the late-night streets.

After a while, inexplicably, the driver says, "We should drop the atom bomb on 'em."

"Every time," says Paul, agreeably.

They alight at a discotheque called The Sensual Experience; the taxi with its mumbling driver moves on. A dim figure awaits them in the doorway with a knife in his hand.

"You can't kill us," says Paul. "We're dead already."

"Paul, be careful, you'll give him a fright," Elsa says.

And indeed the two drugged dilated eyes of the stranger take visible fright as his face comes close to theirs. He gasps and falls to the pavement in a kind of fit. A man comes out of the doorway, looks at the figure on the pavement and turns back in. Elsa and Paul walk away up the street to another discotheque, and by the time they look back a patrol car has found the man on the pavement and the police are hauling him into the back seat.

"There must be something about us," Elsa says. They climb the stairs to Roloff's.

Here they make a decided success. Even Roloff himself

wants to sign them up for a nightly floor show. A sharp-eyed youth with a mass of bushy hair somehow through the clang of the music and the quick bright flicker of multi-coloured lights, notices the fall of Elsa's shadow that crosses with Paul's while they dance. "Look at their dancing shadows!" he tells the crowd. "What have they got there?"

Paul and Elsa soon have a dancing-space to themselves while the others peer closely all round them to find the source of their trick. Those nearest crouch on the floor trying to see what Elsa has got up her skirt to produce this effect.

"Where does she keep it?"—"No, look at her arms, they make a shadow too."—"Is it something to do with him?—What's he doing, then?"—

Roloff the proprietor switches off his flickering psyche-delic apparatus, leaving the room steadily lit by two side-lamps. Still Elsa's shadow dances with Paul's. He backs away, laughing, and lets her dance by herself.

"It's her shadow, it's falling a different way from anyone else's."

There is loud applause, but Paul is looking serious as he sees the eager faces of Kiel and Tylden among the audience.

"Elsa, it's time to go." And still in vain Roloff tries to sign them up for a nightly floor show. "You've definitely got something to offer," he says.

Tylden comes over. "Poppy's downstairs in the Rolls. She couldn't make the stairs," he says.

"We'd better go along with them," Elsa says. "We can't go on like this."

"We can always go home," Paul says, gathering up their coats from the check-room. On the stairway, Kiel tries to block their path. "She's been dancing so hard you couldn't read the secret code on the soles of her shoes," Kiel says.

Paul passes him by and Elsa follows, yawning. "My feet are sore," she says.

They have to walk two blocks for a taxi, while the Rolls circles the block, passing them twice. Princess Xavier can be seen to wave a handkerchief appealingly each time.

"You would think they were alive," says Elsa.

"One can't tell the difference," Paul says.

They go on to Arthur's on the East Side and back downtown to The Throb. To put his mind at ease, at just after three-thirty in the morning, Paul decides to call on Pierre.

"He won't let us in at this hour," Elsa says.

"He can't refuse his mother and his father."

Pierre eventually lets them in with narrowed eyes, pulling his dressing-gown over his thin chest. His friend Peregrine, fully dressed, is working on some papers, and when he sees Pierre's parents, folds them up without a word.

"I hope we're not disturbing you," says Elsa, sitting down.

"I'm just going to get cigarettes from the machine," says Peregrine. He stacks his papers and leaves.

"I was asleep," says Pierre.

The room has been newly decorated with Chinese panels, lacquered furniture, and a screen painted with flat white petals and pink birds. Paul's long fingers trace the carvings of an ivory figurine.

"Do you exist?" Paul says.

"Don't be vulgar," says Pierre.

"Because," says Paul, "your mother and I were killed by a bomb in the spring of 1944. You were never conceived, never born."

"It's rather a personal matter," Pierre says, "isn't it?"

"Really, Paul, I think he's right," Elsa says. "One shouldn't intrude at this hour of the morning."

Pierre smiles. "It's perfectly charming of you to come like this, really. I don't mind a bit."

Outside, they find Peregrine trying to extricate himself from Poppy, who stands on the pavement beside her Rolls, holding him in conversation. "I want to have a word with Pierre's mother," she is saying. "His mother is a very old friend of mine. Do tell her I'm here." The three men and the driver sit in the Rolls solemnly waiting.

"Don't look back or answer her," says Paul as he comes out into the street with Elsa. But Peregrine calls out, "There's a lady here wants to see you, Mrs. Hazlett."

"Walk on, Elsa," says Paul. "Our life's our own to do what we like with."

At the corner of the street they wait till another taxi pulls in to the kerb. They ride off, this time followed closely by the Rolls.

"That car behind us, the Rolls Royce—" Paul says to the driver, "we want it to get lost."

They drive through Central Park, then quickly double back. Paul does a deal with the taxi-driver to wait for them outside Katerina's flat.

"I was asleep," she says. "Did you bring me good news, Pa?"

"Your father just wanted to know if you were alive," Elsa says.

"He could have called me in the morning. Where have you been? It's late."

"We went to L'Étoile and we couldn't get in, then we went to the Banana Skin. We started at Jimmy Ryan's. We got to a golden wedding somewhere, I forget. All over the place."

Paul says, "Do you need some money?"

"You have to be joking," she says.

He takes out his cheque book and, sitting on the arm of a chair, rests it on his knee while he writes out a cheque.

"We still have places to go," he says. "Come on, Elsa."

"Not this late?" Katerina says. She is looking at the cheque, then folds it up. She looks at Elsa. "Do I thank you or Pa?" she says.

"You thank him, I suppose," Elsa says. "I never had any money in my life. It's all a myth."

"You should go home," Katerina says, dopily. "You know, you gave me a fright, waking me up. I almost called the cops. You should let me know before you come on a visit, there might be an inconvenience."

"I did tell your father that," Elsa says, looking at herself as she passes the glass in the hallway. "I told him it was rude."

"Melly," says Paul, "I knew you'd still be up. I hope you don't mind."

"I never go to bed at night," says Melly. "Have a drink. Help yourself."

"Elsa's waiting."

"Where?"

"In the other room. Talking to your night watchman."

"Oh, well."

Melly is shrivelled with a great age. She is alert and heavily laden with bracelets and necklaces. Her hair is brightly gilded, her fingers are long and crooked. She is Paul's oldest friend in New York. Above the Adam fire-

place is the Titian she bought from Paul's family in Montenegro before the war. Her collection of paintings spreads
from room to room throughout her Park Avenue duplex
flat.

"Melly, do you remember those trips I made to New
York, when the war was on?"

"Of course I remember them."

It was Melly who got him the job at Columbia University and kept the apartment on the East River vacant
for him.

"Our apartment's overheated, Melly."

"What can one do? It's an old building. They'll tear it
down like everything else."

"Melly, are you real?"

"Sure I'm real," she says, "and I've got the money to
prove it."

"I get ideas," he says.

"Maybe you're hooked on something," she says. Her
bracelets jingle. "Go get some cognac," she says. Her
fingers reach for a pen on the table by the side of her chair.
She takes up a writing block on which she has made a list.
Paul fetches a tray of cognac and two glasses.

"Doesn't Elsa want a drink? Tell her to come on in."

"No, she said she'd rather wait. I think she's anxious to
get home."

"Well I'll just tell you this," says Melly, "to show
whether I'm alive or not. I'm planning a show of my paintings to raise funds for the Met. I want everyone to come. I
sent a wire to Truman. I sent a cable to Solzhenitsyn but he
didn't answer yet. If he comes I'll serve vodka and caviar,
I guess that's what he's habituated to. I called Peggy in
Venice. I said, 'Look, Peggy, we have to talk.' She just

had a robbery but then I read in the *Times* that she got them all back. I sent a wire to Bertholt Brecht but he didn't answer yet. Here's the list of the names who've answered. It's quite a list."

"Melly, it's time for your rub." It is Melly's nurse at the door of the room holding a bottle of cologne.

"I have to go for my rub-down," Melly says. "I don't go to bed till morning but I have to have my rub at four."

Paul helps her out of the chair and the nurse comes to take her arm. She says, as she walks slowly across the room, "Do the two Rothschilds still go out at four in the morning to give tea from that wagon to these winos in the Bowery?"

"I think they do," he says.

"I saw a movie the other evening. I forgot what it was called. What was it called, Lillian?"

"*The Sacred River*," says the nurse.

Melly says, "All their breasts showing."

"It was bottoms," says the nurse.

"Well it looked like breasts," says Melly.

"How are your feet?" says Paul.

"Not so bad."

They are walking home from Melly's in the morning light. They turn east at Forty-sixth Street. The garbage trucks are out and the early workers are passing them on the pavements.

Paul looks up and down the avenues at each corner. "Poppy and her crowd seem to have given us up," says Paul. "I wonder why?"

"I'll be glad to get home," Elsa says.

They stand outside their apartment block, looking at the

scaffolding. The upper stories are already gone and the lower part is a shell. A demolition truck waits for the new day's shift to begin. The morning breeze from the East River is already spreading the dust.

Elsa stands in the morning light reading the billboard. It announces the new block of apartments to be built on the site of the old.

"Now we can have some peace," says Elsa.

Out of the traffic behind them a voice calls out, "Elsa, Paul—don't keep us waiting any longer."

Poppy is leaning out of the window of the Rolls. The three men are asleep, Kiel beside the driver, Miles Bunting and Tylden in the back, their heads lolling on the puffy leather upholstery of the car.

"We'll take you back. Hurry," Poppy calls.

"Come, Elsa," Paul says, "we can go back with them. They've been very patient, really."

She turns to the car, he following her, watching as she moves how she trails her faithful and lithe cloud of unknowing across the pavement.